SHATTERED TIME

Stephen B. McAfee

ISBN: 978-1-4834-4547-2 (sc)
ISBN: 978-1-4834-4548-9 (e)

Lulu Publishing Services rev. date: 02/17/2016

DEDICATION

This book is dedicated to the family and friends who encouraged me to write another book. A special thank you goes out to Mrs. Pat Reaves for her editing skills, her input and support.

CHAPTER ONE

In the spring of 2001, Joe Adams was exactly where he had always dreamed of being at that stage in his life. He was 60 years old, slightly overweight but in good health. He still had a full head of mostly blond hair with only slight graying around the temples. He was married to his high school sweetheart, Virginia, and together they spent 40 years operating a successful plumbing business. They had a comfortable home in Rock Island Illinois – a city of about 40,000 people. It was situated on the Iowa-Illinois border, separated by the mighty Mississippi River.

That evening, he was alone at their lake property in Leisure Lake Iowa. It was about 60 miles north of their main home in Rock Island. He and Virginia purchased that home a number of years earlier. They bought it so that they could get away from the stresses of the business. It was far away enough that they could get away from the city, yet close enough that it didn't take a long car ride to get there. Over the years, they used it mainly for the weekends, but since retiring they spent much more time there. That night, Virginia had stayed home. She wanted to be part of a 5-mile run, in the city, the next day, while Joe wanted to watch the biggest football game of the year at the cabin, in peace and quiet.

Joe's younger brother, Keith, was coming up to the lake the next morning to go fishing. Keith was actually Joe's half-brother, but the words "half-brother "or "step-father" were not used in their home when they were growing up. They were always a family without divisions. Though the two had different last names, they were brothers through and through. Joe loved and respected his step-father with the same love any boy has for his father. He was the Dad that he didn't have to be, but was. Everything was as it should be, and Joe settled back into his favorite chair for a night of great football.

The game began as all games do with the singing of the National Anthem quickly followed by about five long commercials. These were the same commercials that he had seen many times before. Joe's mind started to wander. Suddenly he realized that he had been reviewing a common theme in his life.

Why is it, Joe asked himself, *that I am thinking about this again? What was it that happened today to make me think about my father again, and about Pearl Harbor, again? The past is the past, it can't be changed....But what if it could? Stop it!"* he scolded. *You've been looking forward to tonight's football game all year. Now just go in the kitchen, make yourself a drink, relax, and enjoy the game. It may have been normal, when you were a child, to fantasize over saving your father, but you're a grown man now. The man who raised you was a wonderful dad to you. He always treated and loved you with the same fervor as he treated and loved Keith. Things happen for a reason..., it was meant to be..., let it go.*

As he began to get up from his easy chair, in front of the TV, a feeling came over him that could only be described as having static electricity consume his body entirely. He felt a little dizzy; off balance, and his eyes seemed to go blank for a moment. As he worked at regaining his balance and control over his body, he suddenly realized that he was no longer in his living room, but somewhere entirely foreign to him. And, he was no longer alone.

"Please don't be afraid," she said. He immediately recognized that voice. It was the velvety and sensual voice that had sent chills up his spine as a youth. It reminded him of Marilyn Monroe. In fact, this woman looked exactly like the most famous sex symbol and movie star of the 1950s. She was blonde, voluptuous, pure of skin and soul, and was smiling that smile that only Marilyn could smile. Chanel #5 was the perfume that she was known to wear, and the room was filled with its wonderful lavender scent. The simple, soft white, dress she wore was the same dress she made famous in the movie *The Seven Year Itch*. Those beautiful, flirtatious eyes gazed at him with warmth and wanting. But it couldn't be. Marilyn Monroe had been dead for close to 50 years. Yet there was no denying that the woman, over whom he had lusted, since he was a boy, was standing right in front of him. The first thing that came into his mind was that he must have just died suddenly. It surprised him that he was suddenly concerned about his physical appearance; yet, he also realized that he was mesmerized and star stuck in the presence of the one and only, Marilyn. He was, at that moment, as captivated as any teenaged girl would be in the presence of a rock star.

Joe forced himself to take his eyes off the woman to try to figure out where he was. He appeared to be in a moderately sized room, in a Victorian-style house. The cool air and soft lighting were the first things he noticed. That environment was obviously designed to make any occupant feel comfortable and relaxed. It was perfectly furnished in a manner that one would expect to see on a southern plantation, or in a northern mansion. Such high, textured ceilings, bordered by wide, polished wood trim that would only be seen in the most expensive of homes, from an earlier time period. There was no ceiling light, but an attractive, antique-style, fan was rotating in a slow, rhythmic manner. The walls of the room were smooth plastered and painted in a clamshell, off-white, color. They blended perfectly with the very large, burgundy window curtains. The same wood trim that adorned the ceiling was used in great abundance to set off the large windows and the mopboard around the floor. Joe noted that there was a large portrait hung over the massive fireplace at one end of the room with two chairs and a couch matching the era and the charm of the room.

In an attempt to regain his composure, he nervously asked, "Where am I? How did I get here? Who are you, really?"

The joy, warmth and sound of glee that came from the beautiful blonde's laughter filled the room like a warm blanket on a cold night. Her allure immediately erased any thoughts in Joe's mind that he was in any type of danger. With an almost giggle mixed in with flirtation in her voice, she responded, "Please don't be afraid. It must be a real shock for you to suddenly be here. I will answer all of your questions in a minute; but first, will you please answer one for me? What's your name?"

Completely consumed by the woman's charm and again feeling comfortable, he told her that his name was Joe Adams.

"I've been around the world three times, to two county fairs, and to a goat rope'n, but I don't know what's happening here. I need some answers. Please tell me what's going on," Joe rattled on like a schoolboy.

"Oh, Joe; you are such a brave man and I need you to know that you have nothing to fear. When I answer your question I know that someone like you will be smart enough to understand," she said in that same calming voice. She gently took Joe's hand and led him to the couch as she began to tell Joe the truth about what was happening.

Calmly and yet boldly she said, "You are on a spaceship, as you earth people like to call it. You will be returned to Earth very soon, unharmed and hopefully glad that you had a chance to be here for a little while. You can leave anytime you wish. If ever you feel frightened, or threatened, you just say that you want to go back and we will return you, unharmed. You are our guest and you will be treated with all of the respect and hospitality that we can give you."

"I can't believe what you're saying," Joe said scornfully. "A spaceship; really…?"

He decided to play along and find out if he'd fallen over from a heart attack and died, which was what he thought might have happened. After all, he had always been a logical man who based his life on reality. Sitting in his living room one moment, and then suddenly transported to a spaceship, of all things, was not reality. He never believed in little green men from Mars or spaceships from outer space. He had about as much faith in those who preached about aliens, as he did in those who believed that magic tricks were real. Still there were those who perpetuated the Roswell conspiracy theory. That happened in the 50's and supposedly a spaceship crashed to Earth, in Roswell, New Mexico. Then the government allegedly covered up that they had recovered an alien body.

"You're not the first to come aboard our ship," she continued. "The pyramids would not have been built, if not for us. Marconi never would have invented the radio, if he hadn't been here. Thomas Edison has been here more than once. Certainly, we had a hand in developing your modern-day computers. Our goal is to give your planet ideas and then see what is made of them. Now we have a plan for you, if you will accept it."

"You mean to tell me that you plucked me from my living room, scared the hell out of me, kept me from the college football game of the year, just so that I, as a plumber, could invent the perfect toilet?" he argued.

Marilyn looked directly into Joe's eyes, and with a more serious tone in her voice, said, "No, Joe. You do have a passion but it is not for inventing the perfect toilet. It is Pearl Harbor. You've never been able to accept that the United States was so unprepared for the Japanese attack; nor how the enemy was able to get so close with their fleet to carry out such a bombing raid. You have struggled with; why the radar man who saw the planes coming, did not react to the threat, and you never have been able to accept how your father could have died there without having a chance to even protect himself."

Joe was so surprised that this woman knew so much about him that he was without thought. And what could he say? He was sure that he had died and this was what happened in the afterlife. There was no other explanation.

"The British actually won the Revolutionary war, but George Washington had more help than most people will ever know. It was because of our help that he was able to change the outcome for the Americans." she said in a very matter of fact way. "And do you really believe that someone like Abraham Lincoln, who failed in everything he ever did, could not only become President of the United States, but become the one person who freed the slaves and changed history without some kind of help? Yes, Mr. Lincoln was a skeptic too, when he came here."

"How is it," Joe asked, "that when we first met, you didn't even know my name; but a few minutes later, you think that you know all about my passions? I'm not a smart man, but you really can't expect me to accept these outlandish things that you're saying. Marilyn Monroe has always been my number one dream woman. I'd do just about anything she asked, but my mind can't go along with this. I'm very suspicious of what you want and why."

"I'm not Marilyn Monroe, Joe; but if you see me as her, that is good because it gives you peace. I could not tell anything about you when you were on Earth. I needed to have personal contact with you before I could read your soul and your mind. I know after being with you a few minutes all I need to know about you."

Marilyn sat back a little to allow Joe some time to absorb what she had said before she continued. "I know that you were born on December 9th, 1941, two days after the bombing of Pearl Harbor. I know that your mother's name was Cora and that she was a nurse in the naval hospital in San Diego, California. I know that your mother and father met and married there. I know that you believe your father was sleeping on the USS Arizona on that Sunday morning when the Japanese attacked and sank that ship. His body was never recovered. You were raised by your mother and your stepfather on a farm in Iowa. You had a good and happy childhood but you hated farming. Soon after graduating from high school, you became an apprentice plumber and afterwards started your own business with your wife. That business grew so that now, at 60 years old, you have let your children run the business. You have always tried to do what is right. You're a good man, husband, and father. But you've always missed your father and dreamt that somehow you could warn the military about what was about to happen at Pearl Harbor. I know that you have always wanted to give your father at least a fighting chance."

"But you can't change history" Joe managed to say.

"We do not change history Joe, just like we didn't change what happened in 1776. We gave George Washington just enough information so that he could change it if he really worked hard at it. We didn't tell Marconi how to invent the radio. We just told him it was possible. You can change what happened at Pearl Harbor but it will cost you much in blood, sweat, and possibly tears. It may be the hardest thing that you've ever done and you will have to do it on your own without our help. So I ask you, Joe, are you interested in giving it a try?"

"Are you telling me that you'll help me go back in time to change what happened at Pearl Harbor?" Joe asked skeptically.

"Not exactly," Marilyn replied, "but time travel is possible and we are willing to help you understand how to do it. If you wish to use it for that purpose, that's up to you."

The shock of what Joe had just heard made him start to shake with excitement and he worried that he was about to have a heart attack, if he were not dead already. But, he then wondered how a 60-year-old man could possibly change what happened so long ago? Where would he find the strength?

"How long do I have to think about this?" he asked. Marilyn quickly answered, "We really do not care if you do this or not. We are interested in seeing the outcome, if you succeed. The choice to do it, or not, is completely yours. If you say yes, we will proceed; if not, we will send you back with no time lost and no memory of this ever having happened."

Joe concluded that he must have fallen asleep and was in the midst of a very realistic dream. The kind of senseless dream where one went to school and forgot to put on his pants. It was as if he was standing in a classroom in his underwear. In that situation, he failed to understand how he could have possibly forgotten to get dressed, as well as how to deal with the situation in which he found himself. No matter what he tried to do in those dreams, things just seemed to go where they would. This was probably the same.

What the hell? Joe decided. *I'll go for it and if it doesn't work out then nothing has changed. I'll probably wake up and be pissed off because I missed the big game.*

Marilyn raised herself from the couch and explained to Joe, "This is not a dream. Dreams do however express people's true feelings. My job is to greet you and to make you feel comfortable. If you had been introduced to the person I am going to have you meet without first being comforted, there might be a problem with you being able to accept it. Now I need to introduce you to someone who will answer all of your questions. He will advise you further on how, or if, you should proceed. Please follow me. He will be introduced to you as Dr. Webster. We realize that you consider the historical Daniel Webster to be the most intelligent man in history. After all he did write the first dictionary. That name should help you respect him for his intellect and authority."

Continuing with what he now was convinced was a dream, Joe stayed back behind Marilyn just far enough so that he could watch her walk, that special way, that only Marilyn Monroe could walk. She seemed unaware of his stare as she led him to a closed door. Before she opened the door, she said to Joe, "The gentleman you are about to meet may look a little strange to you, but don't be alarmed by that. Also, be aware that he does not talk, at least not in the way you are accustomed. He will communicate with you through thought waves. We have learned that people do not always say exactly what they mean but they always mean what they think. Therefore, to avoid any misunderstandings or false statements, it is better to read people's minds than to hear what they have to say."

CHAPTER TWO

Joe was then led into a large room that reminded him of the office of a very successful lawyer. One wall was a bookcase that appeared to be filled from floor to ceiling with the finest literature. At the far end of the room was a large desk, obviously handmade of the finest lumber. The overly-large window behind the desk revealed the image of a large and prosperous city. To the left side of the room was a grand fireplace with a calm welcoming fire. In front of the fireplace were a large overstuffed couch and two overstuffed chairs. A person was sitting on the couch. As Joe entered, the person stood and walked across the room to greet him.

This is just a kid, Joe thought. He was a little more than four and a half feet tall, very skinny with a head that was overly proportioned to the rest of his body. His eyes, too large for his face, were a brilliant shade of blue. His nose was no more than two small holes in his flat face, and he seemed to have no ears. He was completely bald, and his skin was a pale shade of green. As the stranger came near, he extended his right hand. Joe noted that it only had three fingers, and a thumb; similar to what one might see when looking at a cartoon figure in a parade.

A loud, baritone pitched voice, entered Joe's mind saying, *"My name is Dr. Webster...it's very nice to meet you Mr. Adam. Please come in, and have a seat."*

Although warned by Marilyn, Joe was in such shock and disbelief that his mind went completely blank. He just stared at the strange looking stranger with no form of thought. After a few long minutes, Joe regained his composure and took the strangers hand in a very weak handshake. Dr. Webster led Joe to one of the chairs in front of the fireplace, opposite the couch.

I assure you, sir that I am not a cartoon character and I am not a 'kid' as you put it. I am in fact a great deal older than you are. I am also aware of the discomfort you are feeling at this moment. Please let me assure you that although thinks may seem strange to you, there is no danger here to you. Joe heard in his mind.

"I'm sorry if I appear to be rude." Joe managed to say. "But yes, I am very upset about all of this. I hear your voice and yet you are not talking."

Dr. Webster explained to Joe that he was totally deaf, because his people no longer used the spoken word. Through evolution they had lost their ears and vocal cords. He told Joe that if it was more comfortable for him to speak using words, that he could do so; but Dr. Webster would hear him through his thoughts, which might be different from what he was saying.

There are no liars, cheats or phonies here, Mr. Adams. So let us now discuss the purpose for which you were summoned. The words clearly formed in Joe's brain, but no words were spoken. Dr. Webster was indicating enough had been said about the language issue.

Changing the subject abruptly, Dr. Webster continued, *it would appear that you have this obsession or idea causing you much preoccupation over the sneak attack and subsequent bombing of Pearl Harbor, resulting in the death of your father. It is your belief that the unfortunate occasion on December 7, 1941, deprived you of being raised by your natural father. It is your conviction that your father was asleep in his makeshift bed below deck on that early Sunday morning; and therefore, never had a chance to even defend himself when that ship was sunk by a Japanese torpedo. You desire to go back in time to correct what you consider to be that injustice, and to warn the government of the events before they occur. Am I accurate in my evaluation of these specifics Mr. Adams?*

"Yes" was the only response that Joe could get out before Dr. Webster interrupted him and began again. *It is very possible to travel in time but only backward. It is not possible to travel forward to a time zone that has yet to exist. There are many things that you do not know and have not considered about what you desire. For example, any change you make in the past will affect the present, no matter how diminutive you may think that change may be. What you deem to be fact or historical truth about the past may not be accurate or completely true. There are many things you could not change about the past even if you wanted to do so. For example,-perhaps your great-grandmother had an unwanted encounter with a man when she was a young girl. Let's say that as a result of that incident, your great-grandmother became pregnant and gave birth to your mother. You could not go back in time and stop the incident because if the pregnancy did not ensue, your mother would not have been born; and therefore, you would not be present. If you didn't exist, you could not stop that event from happening. You would cease to exist at that moment and the future would be distorted forever. Do you understand Mr. Adams?*

Frustrated, Joe barked back, "I don't know what you're talking about! I'm not trying to stop some guy from having a jump in the hay with my Grandmother. I just want to stop Pearl Harbor from happening, in the way it did. I want to give those people, who died there, a chance to fight back, a warning of what was about to happen and then let whatever happens… well, let it be."

Dr. Webster paused for a moment and then said; *Let me put this in a more personal perspective. Let's say that you are successful in your endeavor and that you successfully warn everyone involved and your father survives that assault. Your life would change expediently and you may be personally disappointed in the outcome. You would not be wedded to your wife because you almost certainly would not have met her. Your children would not ever have been born. Your half-brother and half-sister would not be alive because your mother would not have married your stepfather. Are you sure that you want to exchange the existence of your children for the life of your father? Your father may or may not have been the great father to you that your stepfather was. He might have been a drunk and wife beater, for all you know. These are things that you need to evaluate before you embark on the serious adventure you so deeply believe that you wish to pursue. I have given you some ideas to contemplate; now it is time for you to decide. If you agree to move forward with this plan, you will depart here with only an elementary knowledge of how to build a time machine mechanism. That device could allow you to see and possibly effect the past. What you so powerfully wish to change could then be accomplished. If you are still solemn about building it, you can; but it will take a lot of hard work on your part. We give you the design, we give you the fundamentals, but you need to figure out how to make it work.*

Without giving much consideration to the sober things that Dr. Webster had said, Joe said robustly, "Let's do it! After all this was some kind of a dream anyway… it had to be."

Very well Dr. Webster said. *There could be a great deal of danger to your planet if things are not done correctly. We will therefore be monitoring your movements but we will only interfere if necessary. Now, I will send you back to the time and place from where you came here.*

Suddenly, Joe felt that same static electricity which he felt earlier, consume his body. Only a moment past until he lost all memory of the adventure that he had just been on. As he sat back in his easy chair, he was kind of glad that his wife couldn't come up to the lake this weekend. He missed her when she wasn't around, but he knew that although she would sit and watch the game with him, she really did not like football.

Joe and Virginia had been married for forty-five years and they had two children. Their daughter, Kathryn and son, Robert now ran the successful plumbing business that he and Virginia had spent years building. Joe felt great satisfaction in knowing that someday his children would be as comfortable in life as he was. This was the life he had always wanted.

CHAPTER THREE

In the early evening of December 9, 1941, in a room at Balboa Naval Hospital, San Diego, California; Cora Adam's stared, in loving marvel, at the bundle sucking at her breast. She had spent so many months in absolute apprehension over what this baby would look like. But at that moment, it simply did not matter. She understood, what a mother's love really meant. She had never felt those awe-inspiring feelings for any living thing. If this baby had been born with green and purple spots on his face, she knew she would still feel the same way. All of the things that had happened over the past nine months, all the tears, all the fears and all the heartbreak, meant nothing to her at that moment.

"Mommy's little Joe," she whispered down at him. "I can't believe that yesterday I didn't want you and today I would die for you. If only Jerry could see you now. He would have to love you as I do. Maybe, just maybe, he would love me again, too."

Cora's one-sided conversation with her newborn son was overheard by her best friend, Naomi Malani. Both women were nurses at this hospital but right then Cora was a patient and Naomi was on duty. Her starched white uniform complemented her 5'4 smart figure perfectly. Her jet black hair was styled in a short, de-a cut. Naomi's luminous, black round eyes with natural tan skin; completed a vision of a beautiful Italian woman. This made her the resentment of many women. But she didn't seem to realize how stunning she was. Her Texan drawl, and frank no-nonsense character, was charismatic to many and a threat to others.

"He is so beautiful," Naomi said, "and it is so nice to see happiness in your face again. I haven't seen you look so good for so long... you deserve to be this happy."

Cora did not really want to hear anything that might pull her away from the ecstasy she was feeling for her new baby, but she had to ask, "Have you heard anything about Jerry?"

"No, sweetie," Naomi answered; "The Arizona took a direct hit and there was an awful explosion. I hear that maybe as many as a thousand men died on that ship. I hate to give you this news on this grand day but I knew that you'd want to know. I don't like Jerry. He's all broth and no beans, but I hope that he's okay for your sake. If it were up to me, I'd break his nose so bad that he'd lose it if he sneezed."

Cora knew how Naomi felt about Jerry and why. "He will change Naomi. As soon as he sees little Joe, he will change," Cora insisted.

Naomi always spoke what was on her mind, usually without thinking first. "He'll take one look at that little fella," replied Naomi, "and know that he didn't sire him. That won't make things better between you two. It'll just make 'em worse."

Without looking up, Cora insisted "He will change Naomi. You'll see... you just wait... you'll see."

Naomi convinced Cora to let her take little Joe back to the nursery. She was right. With everything that had happened the past few days, Cora was both physically and emotionally exhausted and really did need to sleep.

For months Cora had tried to forget the assault, the face of the man who raped her and prayed that the baby she was carrying was Jerry's and not the blonde headed monster's. When Jerry got home that day, just a few minutes after Cora, he saw the bruises, the torn clothes, the tears and the shame she felt. There was no hiding what had happened, but instead of offering comfort and reassurance that she so desperately needed, Jerry blamed her. The man, who had shown her unconditional love, now had only contempt for her. Her only hope was that the baby would be a boy with black hair and dark skin. Then, maybe, Jerry would remember that he wanted a boy so badly and they would be a family. But she knew that Naomi was right. Jerry would never accept this blonde-haired, fair-skinned, baby and she knew that their marriage was probably over. While she was pregnant, she had considered giving the baby up for adoption if it wasn't Jerry's. But as soon as she held him in her arms, she knew that she couldn't give up her baby. Even if she did, Jerry would never accept her and love her the way he once did. She never dreamed that she could love anyone more than her husband, but this baby proved her wrong.

And then, there was Jerry's mother. She was old-school Japanese and made it very clear that Caucasians were an undesirable race of people. She was furious with Jerry when he married Cora. Jerry had told Cora that he knew his mother would come around when their Japanese son was born. "We will need to raise him in the ways of my people" he would say.

His mother certainly did not attempt to hide the fact that she only married a Japanese-American sailor to become an American citizen. Cora had witnessed Jerry's mother treat his step-father with total distain. The story she heard was that his mother and Jerry, her three-year-old son, came to America together after Jerry's mother and step-father were married in Japan the previous year. The fact that Jerry was devoted to his mother really didn't matter to Cora. She was confident that the devotion he felt for his mother would transfer to her once they were married. And yet, something did not seem natural. *It was probably just the silly fears of a young bride,* she told herself.

On the cab ride from the hospital to Cora's apartment, Naomi begins to talk randomly, "I know that ya don't know if you're a-washin' or a-hangin'. It's hard for you to know what to do now that Jerry is supposed dead. With the war being declared and the Navy being so shorthanded, Jerry won't be able to come stateside, even if he is alive. It's going to be hard for you to go back to work and take care of the little critter, too. But you know you need to work to pay the bills. I was just thinking that maybe I could bunk in with you, for a bit. I work nights and you work days, I can take care of the little fella while you're at work, and we could share expenses. Ya don't need to answer me now, but think about it. I could be as handy as hip pockets on a hog."

With equal parts of anger and appreciation, Cora said, "Jerry's not dead. He'll be alright. I know that the communication between Hawaii and the States is a problem right now, but I'll hear from him."

"I know honey, I'm sure your right" Naomi says. "Just keep what I said in mind."

Cora insisted on believing the things that she had been telling herself, until the day the yellow cab came. Naomi had come over to check on Cora and little Joe. They were discussing the women they knew who had been notified by the Navy that their men had been killed at Pearl Harbor. There were so many dead soldiers, and so few command vehicles, that the officers notifying the loved ones were forced to use yellow cabs. Yellow cab, after yellow cab, would come to the families' homes and an officer would walk to the front door. Everybody knew what that meant! "Let the yellow cab pass by my house," was the prayer of every mother, wife and sweetheart who saw them coming down their street. But on that day the cab did not pass by Cora's house. It stopped.

Cora watched the lips move on the officer who was speaking, but she did not seem to hear anything. She knew that he was telling her that her husband was missing, and presumed dead, but she just did not hear the words. It was as though all of her senses had failed her, at that moment. She felt no emotion of sorrow, anger, or fear. She felt absolutely nothing. She had no emotion in her voice as she thanked them for notifying her, and assured them that she was all right.

When the men left, Cora turned to Naomi and said, "Please don't say anything right now. I hope you understand that I just want to be alone, for a little while."

After Naomi left, Cora fixed herself a cup of tea. As she sipped on it, reality began to fill her mind. Her mother had died giving birth to her. She never knew who her father was. She was raised in an orphanage. She just couldn't and wouldn't subject any child of hers to that type of childhood. It was her and little Joe now. She would do whatever she needed to do, to protect him from the shame and hardship, with which she was raised. Her baby was a blue eyed, blonde headed, fair skinned boy. Her husband had dark skin, with coal black hair and eyes. If Joe did not know what his father looked like, he would never have to question why he didn't look like him. He'd never need to know that Jerry wasn't his father nor that he was conceived in a dirty back alley in San Diego. He could worship and honor his father as all little boys should. She would tell little Joe how much his father loved him that he was a hero, who died for him and for his country. The only one who knew the truth is Naomi. So Cora decided right then and there, that she had to end her friendship with her. She hated that thought but for the sake of her baby, she would!

Cora spent the next hours, going through the apartment, finding every picture of Jerry. She tenderly held in her hands: his military picture that hung on the wall, their wedding picture that she cherished so much, and the picture of her and Jerry at the San Diego Zoo. She remembered that Jerry had talked a total stranger into taking it for them. Every picture of Jerry was placed in a pile on the coffee table. With scissors in hand and tears running down her face; she cut up each picture and put them in the garbage. Suddenly, the phone rang. Cora was crying so hard that she could hardly speak, when she answered it.

"Hello dear," were the words that came from the phone; "I just called to make sure that you're all right" said Naomi.

"This poor, pathetic woman and her bastard son don't need your pity" Cora yelled at Naomi through the mouthpiece. "You think you know everything about everybody and how they should live. I don't need some woman who can't even get a man of her own to tell me how I should run my life."

"I'm fix'en to come over there right now" Naomi shot back. "Don't you dare try to keep me out, I'll kick down your damn door if I have to, but you're goanna talk to me."

Knowing that Naomi would do just that, Cora had no alternative but to tell Naomi of her plan. Feeling defeated, she opened the door and let her in. "You're the only one who can ruin this for me, so please understand, I need to give up my best friend in the world for my son" Cora explained to Naomi.

Without even having to think about what she just heard, Naomi said, "You're the finest person I've ever met. I don't agree with you at all. Ya can't hide or run away from your problems. They always come back to haunt ya; but if you've made up your mind and think this is best, I'll support ya. Your secrets are mine."

Within a few days, the decision was made that living together, sharing expenses, and one watching Joe while the other one worked, was in everyone's best interest. As Naomi carried boxes into Cora's apartment, she told Cora that they would make it; this was what was best for all three of them.

"It ain't plum but pert near" she said. "Just wait till you meet my brother. He helped me load these boxes into my car but he couldn't come over to meet you. I don't know why. He's good looking with blonde hair, beautiful blue eyes and big muscles; you'll love him when you meet him."

Cora assumed that Naomi's brother must have taken his looks after her German mother's side of the family because of his fair complexion, and that she took after her Italian father.

Naomi just seemed to be the perfect fit for Cora. She was straight talking, honest and sometimes crusty, but Cora found security in having her near. Naomi loved little Joe so much that Cora was surprised, at times, how this hard talking, hard hearted woman could have so much love to give.

One day, as they were together, Naomi answered the ringing phone and said, "Hi Mom, how ya'll doing?"

Instantly, the color faded from Naomi's face. Cora suddenly noticed Naomi's knees weaken and a look of absolute terror came over her face. Naomi dropped the phone and slid down onto the floor.

Cora dashed over to Naomi and asked, "What's going on?"

Naomi was unable to speak. Cora picked up the receiver of the phone and yelled, "What's the matter?"

On the other end of the phone was Naomi's sobbing mother. She told Cora that Naomi's brother had been in a car accident and was dead.

Cora went with Naomi to the funeral home. She walked behind Naomi as they approached the casket. She knew how close Naomi was to her brother and wanted to be right beside her, if she collapsed when she saw her beloved brother's body. Naomi had recovered from her initial shock and had again regained her strong persona. She kissed her fingers and touched the forehead of the cold body before her.

Then for the first time, Cora saw Naomi's brother. Even with his eyes closed, as if he were asleep, Cora knew that she was looking into the face of the man who had raped her. The fair skin, the blonde hair, even with his eyes closed, she knew they were blue. Taken by total shock, Cora froze for a moment, then regained her thoughts and promised herself that she would never tell Naomi, nor anyone else, what she knew to be true. She would let the truth die with him.

CHAPTER FOUR

After the plane landed at the Nagasaki Airport in Japan, Jerry Adams gleefully hugged his mother.

"We have much to be proud of," he told her. "The lazy and stupid Americans have learned what it means to insult the emperor."

"My only child," his mother replied, "your ancestors will be so proud of you, and victory for the emperor is at hand."

She again explained to Jerry what she had told him before, that after the death of Jerry's father; she had married an American-Japanese sailor who was in Japan. They had left their beloved Japan, and moved to America with him. He had legally adopted Jerry, at his mother's insistence. With the American name, Jerry would be looked at with less mistrust, for who would ever think that a person with the last name of Adams could ever be a spy?

"Everyone on this airplane worked very hard for a long time to send information back to Japan so that we would be successful when the attack came. Now it's time for us to rejoice. Your grandparents are excited to see you and we will be living with them. Nagasaki is now our home and we will dwell in the spirits of our ancestors forever."

"I know, Mother," Jerry said, "that when I married Cora, you were disappointed and I didn't want to do it. I never cared for her but I believed it would be easier for me to be accepted by the other sailors on the ship, if I was married to an American. It permitted me to go places and do things that I would not have been able to do if they had any feeling that I might not be totally loyal or really an American. We needed the information I got from the Navy to help with the assault.

And you know, Mother, that I could never accept a half-white child. I only wish that both she and her baby were in Hawaii and had died from the bombs."

On the other side of the world, Jerry met his grandparents for the first time. He wasn't surprised that his Grandmother spoke very little to his mother, never made eye contact with either him or his Grandfather, and that she walked behind them as an act of respect. He had been taught that women were totally subjugated by men, in the Japanese culture, but he had never seen his mother act that way before. She was always so strong minded and independent. He was shocked to see her follow in the ways of her mother, once she was in Japan.

Jerry's grandfather was a conversationalist. In fact, he never seemed to stop talking. He often spoke so fast that Jerry had trouble keeping up with what he was saying. Jerry believed that he spoke Japanese well, because that was the main language of the people with whom he grew from childhood. But now, he was having trouble following everything his grandfather was saying. He knew that his grandfather was much energized about the conquest Japan had over the Americans. He seemed to go on and on, about how proud he was of Jerry, for the information that he and the others sent back to Japan. This helped make the attack such a successful accomplishment. Jerry noted that his grandfather never gave his mother any credit even though she was the ring leader of the whole operation in Hawaii.

Jerry lay on a mat at his grandparent's house and allowed himself a few minutes to let his true feelings come to the surface. Maybe it was the long flight from Hawaii to Japan or maybe it was the strong drinks that his grandfather kept insisting he drink, but he was in turmoil. Maybe it was the reality of what had just happened and wondering how it happened the way it did, or maybe, it was just pure guilt for what his beloved Cora and his country had just gone through. His loyalties between families, cultures and lifestyles, were crushing him on the inside, but he had to maintain his composure on the outside.

"I tried to stop it; I tried to tell them it was coming." He said under his breath. "I deceived my beloved mother, and her friends, but it happened anyway. Why didn't they listen to me? Didn't they get my messages?"

Now he could only continue to do what he had to do for his country. "Oh, Cora, I love you and hope that someday you won't hate me, for what I had to do. I am so sorry that our child will never know that I had to choose between him and our country."

As Jerry drifted off to sleep, he kept wondering how that happened. It didn't make sense because the Japanese code was broken. The Americans knew they were coming. They knew where the Japanese fleet was located. They had to have seen the fleet of over a hundred planes coming on the radar screen. They knew it all. It was almost as if the American military was helping the Japanese. Even after they knew what was going to happen, they put their battleships in a row in Pearl Harbor so they could be picked off, like ducks on a pond. They did the same thing with their planes, at the air base. Everyone in the military knew that you never do something like that. *What happened?*

I have been promised, by my grandfather, that I will be given a high-ranking job in the Japanese government. So now, maybe I can do whatever I can and give information to the Americans about what is going on, when I know it. It will take me a while to get used to everyone calling me by my given name, Takeo Yosohikawa.

CHAPTER FIVE

Joe watched the football game with great enthusiasm, which was kind of odd because the game was very one-sided from the beginning. He usually fell asleep in his chair in the middle of a game like this. It was supposed to be such a great game, but his side was losing badly and he was bored. Tonight he seemed more insightful than usual, and his mind was racing. The game didn't get over until almost 11, and most nights, he was asleep on the couch by nine. When he finally did go to bed, he lay there wide awake.

He started thinking again, as he has done so many times before, about how nice it would be if he could somehow go back to 1941 and warn the military that the Japanese were about to attack. But on this night, the bed on which Jerry usually found so much comfort, felt like a cement slab.

Maybe if I get up and have another drink I'll be able to sleep, he considered. He needed to get some rest because, early the next day, his younger brother, Keith, was coming over so they could go fishing.

Keith was an electronics expert. He had enough college degrees to cover a wall and he had a high raking job with the government as an Electronics Engineer. It seemed like Keith had always been the brains of the family. He was always messing with electronic gadgets and reading the latest gizmo books. Other than computers or other electronic devices, Keith loved fishing. Joe enjoyed being with him in the boat and watching his excitement when he caught a fish, whether it was a keeper or not.

The illumination on the closed curtains against the sliding glass door, told Joe that Keith had pulled into the driveway. He quickly looked at the clock on the wall and realized it is 5:30. He had been sitting there all night. *How stupid*, he thought. One drink to help him sleep turned into four or five, maybe more. Joe hated to drink too much. Then he realized that he was expected to go fishing, and knew that he is in no shape to sit in a rocking boat all day.

Joe greeted Keith at the door. "Come in, little brother. I'm not ready. Fix some coffee will ya, while I jump in the shower real quick?"

Joe showered, changed clothes and when he returned, he found Keith sitting at the kitchen table absorbed with the note pad, on which Joe had been doodling. He was so engrossed that he didn't notice Joe for a moment; but when he did, he blurted out with great enthusiasm, "Who the hell drew this?"

Taken by surprise by Keith's reaction, Joe said "Oh that's just something I was fiddling with last night. I couldn't sleep so I sat there just thinking and started doodling."

Keith recognized the drawing as an electronic schematic that most experts in that field couldn't read, let alone draw.

"You can't even program your VCR, and you're telling me that you drew this?" Keith barked. "There are components here that you have no idea what they are or what they do; and yet, you have identified them and they work perfectly in this, this thing." Keith said excitedly.

Then in a more calm tone and almost as if he were talking to himself he remarked, "Ya know, I did see something like this at the electronics engineers' convention in Las Vegas, last year. Scientists were working on a device to transport solid objects from one place to another in an instant by de-materializing them and then re-materializing them in another place. They claimed that their device could move a solid object from New York to Paris, instantly. They could only transport non-living objects in this manner. When they tried to transport live objects, all they got at the end was dust. First, they tried to transport a flower and all they got in Paris was dust; and the same thing happened when they tried it with a mouse. This drawing is similar to that device but there are some minor differences."

Keith continued to study the drawing intensely. He pointed his finger at part of the drawing and asked Joe, "What is this component here?"

"It's a quantum gravity eraser" Joe blurted out without thinking, in a much more sheepish voice then he had intended.

"There is no such thing. That's impossible. What do you know about quantum gravity anyway?" said Keith.

Getting a little agitated by Keith's attitude, Joe responded sharply "Really, how many times have you told me that nothing's impossible? I don't know why I called it that. It just came to me."

"So that is why you didn't name it because there is no such thing. I can't believe that I'm talking electronics with a plumber." Keith yelled at Joe.

"I didn't leave that on the table for you to get mad at me. You don't need to talk to me like I'm stupid. You came up here to go fishing. So let's go fishing and forget about this thing." Joe snapped back.

In a much calmer voice, Keith said, "We can't go fishing now. It started to rain and you know that I don't fish in the rain. Tell me, Joe, what is this drawing supposed to be?"

Joe reluctantly told Keith about his dream of building a time machine that would allow him to go back in time and change history. "Like... warn the military about the attack coming to Pearl Harbor before it happened" he said, as if it were a passing thought "I don't know where the idea of that drawing came from, but I think it could allow a person to travel in time."

"Listen," Keith said, "it's currently unknown whether the laws of physics would allow time travel into the past. Such backward time travel would have the potential to create a paradox related to causality. Causality is the relativity of an action on a second action. For example, if you were able to take the action to warn the American military of the impending attack, your natural father's life, as well as the lives of many other men, would be saved. That action would change the present which would be the second action. If time travel were possible, don't you think that people from the future would be here now?"

"What makes you so sure that they're not?" Joe responded with some defiance in his voice.

Without responding to Joe's question, Keith says "I need to go home and think about this concept. Can I take the drawing with me so that I can study it more closely?"

CHAPTER SIX

It had been a couple of weeks since Joe heard from Keith and he began to wonder if he should call him to see why. Usually Keith came up to the lake about every weekend to help Joe cut the grass. He used that excuse to go fishing afterwards. So on that Saturday morning as Joe sat on his John Deere tractor cutting grass, he saw Keith's car suddenly pull into the driveway.

"Okay, I built it" he said. "I had a lot of trouble finding some of the parts... and that thing you called a gravity eraser, was something else. I built this control myself. But it was brilliantly designed. It is small, portable, battery powered and about the size of a pack of cigarettes. The best part is that it's got a GPS feature and a calendar that can be set for the day, year and even the minute. I still don't know how the thing is supposed to work or if it will at all. You wanted it, so let's try it out."

Joe was astonished. "Are you crazy? I just couldn't sleep and I was doodling something as I sat at the kitchen table with no real thought in mind. Now you think you built a time machine based on nothing more than that? It was nothing more than scribbling from a man who couldn't sleep"

"Ya, I'm probably crazy. But allow me to be stupid for a minute. This thing is really a work of art. I'm not sure how you figured it out, but you did. Now that I built it, let's turn it on and see what happens."

"Okay" Joe says still unbelieving that Keith had built a time machine. "But don't get mad at me if it does nothing."

Joe led Keith to the basement work shop where Joe thought might be a good place to see if it worked. Joe placed a wooden lawn chair in the middle of the room, took the device from Keith while asking, "How does this thing work?"

"Hell, I don't know." Keith snapped back. "You designed it, you figure it out."

The device was just a little bit smaller than a Television remote, slightly thinner and somewhat shorter. It had a key pad with numbers and letters on it. Joe noticed that it had a recall button which Joe hoped was there so that a person could get back to the present, whenever he wanted, or needed, to do so. Joe saw the power on and off button, a date button, and a location button.

"Do you have a broom and dust pan?" asked Keith.

"Why?" Joe says puzzled.

Keith reminded Joe about the device that he saw at the Las Vegas convention. He told Joe that this device was real close to what he saw there. The other device turned living objects into dust and if Joe was turned into dust, he would need something to clean up the mess.

"And if you are successful at saving your real father's life, then you will need it to clean up my dust." he said. "Think about it. If your real father survives, I, as your half-brother, probably will not have been born! Your children will not exist. Your wife will potentially not be your wife. This great life that you now have will be different; possibly better, although I can't imagine how it could be better. Just keep in mind that it could also be a lot worse. The present may be a lot different than it is now and you might need to clean up a lot of dust."

Joe's mind now was almost a total blur. Never had he thought about how things would be different, if his father had survived that attack.

"I don't know what the past would have been like if my father had survived but I do know what my past has been. If I change the past and save my father's life, does it mean that I am responsible for the outcome of the lives of people I love so much?" The question was overwhelming with all of its consequences.

In an effort to give him self some time to think about the implications of doing such a thing, Joe suggested "Let's just do a few experiments, for now, and see what happens."

Joe took the little gold fish bowl that he had in his work shop and placed it on the wooden lawn chair that he had set in the middle of the room. He pushed the "on" button on the device. The screen on the front of the device lit up and read, "Beginning location." Joe keyed in his zip code and the screen immediately asked for a street address. The screen then asked for a destination. Joe typed in the same information that he put in for the beginning location, insuring that the gold fish bowl would not leave the workshop. Next the screen asked for the "destination date." Joe put in the current date, and when it asked for a time, Joe typed in ten minutes earlier than the present time.

"Are you ready?" Joe asked excitedly.

"Honestly, I don't think this thing will do anything except maybe change the channel on your television." Keith joked.

Joe pointed the device at the fish bowl and hit the enter button. Nothing happened!

Joe and Keith both stared at the chair in disbelief. They turned and faced each other with their open mouths and total blank looks on their faces.

"Wow!" joked Joe. "Did you put batteries in this thing?"

"Don't be silly, of coarse I did. This is unreal." Keith says puzzled that it didn't work.

They realized, at the same time, that they hadn't spoken, but each one knew what the other was thinking. Suddenly, the door to the workshop swung open Joe and Keith watched as the likeness of the both of them enters the workshop. They watched as everything that had happened ten minutes before, was replaying in front of their eyes. The men who entered the workshop didn't see them. They didn't know that they were there. Joe and Keith were in, what seemed to be, an out of body experience. They tried hollering at them. Kevin even tried to touch the people in the room, to get them to see that they were there, but nothing worked. They watched as the image of Joe walked over to the shelf where the gold fish bowl was sitting. They helplessly observed him pick it up and place it on the wooden chair in the room. They heard everything that the two men said, up to the point where they pushed the enter button. Suddenly, before their eyes, they watched, as the two men disappeared.

They were back in the present and discovered that no time had elapsed. The fish bowl was back on the chair and they were staring at it. After a long silence, Joe broke the silence.

"Well this was a learning experience that I didn't expect. But I guess we now know that we can put the broom and dust pan away."

Keith was in a more sober mood than Joe seemed to be. "Why did we think that pointing this thing at the gold fish bowl would affect it only? We went back in time as did the whole room for ten minutes. We were not physical beings any longer but more like spirits or ghosts. It was more like what scientists call Astor-projection. In near death experiences, people talk about floating above their bodies and experiencing everything that is going on around them. This was like that. My mind can't process what I know I've just been through."

"This is not what I expected either." Joe said. "I am not sure what I expected to happen but it wasn't that. I didn't think we would see ourselves, or not be seen by anyone."

"I would never have believed that time travel was possible," Keith admitted. "I never expected to be a part of it, but I was... and I know what happened here, really did happen. I am so excited that I can't control myself."

"I felt like a ghost," Joe said, "Just watching what was happening and not being able to be seen or heard by the people around us. It was spooky."

"It appears that a time traveler can observe the past but can't affect or change it." Keith said. "If that is true, you could go back and watch the attack on Pearl Harbor but you can't change it, or stop it. But this was our first try, we might be able to do more the more we learn."

Somewhat disappointed Joe said, "It looks like you're right. It would still be interesting to go back, and see exactly what happened. It would be cool to at least see what my father looked like, and find out what he was like."

"Some information would need to be obtained. You would have to know your mother's address, when your father was on leave, so that you could see your mother and father together.

"Since Mom died two years ago, how could we get that information?" Joe asked.

"Aunt Naomi is still alive. She is still sharp as a tack and she knew everything. We can ask her." Keith answered.

"Another thing that you may need to consider is what are you going to tell your wife? I think that she will go ballistic about this idea."

Joe hadn't thought about telling his wife anything about the time machine. He didn't know that Keith was going to be able to build one or that it would work.

"She would just think I was crazy." Joe says timidly. "I think that we will just mess with this thing up here at the lake, at times when she isn't here, for now. We don't know how to answerer any question she would have or get her upset by saying anything about this."

CHAPTER SEVEN

Aunt Naomi was really not Joe's and Keith's aunt. She was more like a nanny and lifelong friend to Cora. She lived with the family for all of the boys' lives, and remained living with their mother and father even after "the boys" as she called them, had married and left home. It was just a natural thing for them. It was mom, dad and Aunt Naomi. She was always a little peculiar and demanded respect which she always got along with the love of the family. She was especially helpful when Keith's dad died and it was good to have her there, at that time.

When their mother died, she left Aunt Naomi the house and everything in it. None of the kids had any problem with that at all. She was still living in that house. Both Joe and Keith felt like she was their second mother. The two men pulled into Naomi's driveway just as she is returning from her daily jog.

As they greeted her on the front porch, Joe said, "Don't you think that you're getting a little old to be jogging?"

"Nice to see y'all too," Naomi snapped back in her quick witted tone. "I'll have you boys know that I still go to the gym and exercise three times a week. I swim, play golf and have a little shot of Irish whiskey every day. I can still paddle you boys' butts any time I need to, and don't you forget it."

"Yes ma'am," Joe said respectfully. "Don't get your bloomers in a bunch. We just came over to see how you're doing, or if you need anything."

"No you didn't. You guys look like a fox caught in a hen house. You're up to some sort of mischief, just like when you were kids. Y'all could fool your mamma but you never could fool me! So let's stop walking around the hog pen and get to the point."

Keith and Joe looked at each other and realized that they hadn't thought this through very well. They could not tell her the truth. She would think they were both crazy. They dared not lie to her because that would be like spitting into the wind. It would just comeback and hit them in the face. Keith wondered if they could tell her part of the truth and just leave the time machine part out.

"Joe just wants to find out something's about his natural father," Keith stated truthfully.

"I don't speak ill of the dead," Naomi blurted out.

"What do you mean by that?" Joe jumped in. "You didn't like my father?"

Realizing that she spoke before she thought which she did a lot, Naomi tried to cover herself by changing the subject. "Your mama told you everything about your father. She told you that he was a hero who died in the war. Your momma told you everything else that you need to know. I can't tell you any more than that. She knew him better than I did, so just let it go!"

"Whenever I tried to ask her about him, she was evasive like maybe it was too hard for her to talk about. I don't even know what he looked like. Mom always said that all of the pictures of him had been destroyed and I have always had a problem with that."

Naomi took a step back, looked Joe straight in the eye and yelled, "DON'T YOU DARE CALL YOUR MOTHER A LIAR! She was the finest person I've ever known, and you're not too old to get your face slapped!"

Keith jumped in and said, "He didn't mean it the way you took it, Aunt Naomi. Let me just ask you this: We know that mom and Joe's dad lived in San Diego when they were married, can you remember the address?"

"There is nothing wrong with my memory," Naomi barked back. "It was 12704 Apache Lane, Apartment Four."

"That's all we really wanted to know, Aunt Naomi." Keith said.

"What do you mean that's all you wanted to know? What possible difference would it make to know the address where they lived? But that's good," she responded, "Cause I'm late for my yoga class. Come, give me a kiss goodbye, you tadpoles, and don't forget my birthday is next week. I'm expecting another surprise party."

"Yes ma'am," the two men said at the same time. They then hugged and kissed the woman that they both loved so much.

"Don't you boys go jumping head first into some shallow fish pond! I don't know what you varmints are up to, but make sure ya check the water level first before ya jump off of solid ground," Naomi warned, as the two headed for the car.

"Yes ma'am," they hollered back respectfully.

"Well, that didn't get us very much," Joe said, as the two drove back to Joe's house.

"It got us enough," Keith responded confidently. "It tells us where mom and your real dad lived. It gives an address to put into the time machine."

"But San Diego is a long way from Pearl Harbor and that's where I want to go," Joe murmured under his breath.

"Think about it, Joe. You can't just jump into the attack. You've got to get some background. We need to experiment a little more before we make the big move. You don't just put in a sewer line before you check the condition of the ground, and we need to take this slow."

Back at Joe's kitchen table, Keith said, "We need to evaluate, elaborate, and enumerate on what we have learned so far."

Joe humorously replied "Why don't we just talk it over, Keith?"

Without acknowledging Joe's remark, Keith continued, "The first thing we need to do is isolate the area in which this time travel will work. In our first experiment, our intention was to have just the goldfish bowl go back in time, not the whole room. But I think I know how to solve that problem."

The two men went to the workshop again. This time, Keith walked over to the broom closet and emptied everything out. Then he placed the wooden chair in the broom closet along with the goldfish bowl.

"Now we can leave all of the readings on the machine the same. I see that it has a time delay. We'll put 15 seconds in there, hit the enter button, and leave the machine in the room with the goldfish. If my calculations are correct, only the goldfish bowl will travel in time, not us. Then in ten minutes, it will come back to the present."

"It seems to be too easy," Joe said, "but let's try it." Keith pushed the "enter" button, placed the machine on the chair next to the goldfish bowl and closed the door.

Both men watched the now empty shelf where the goldfish bowl had been before they moved it. They really did not expect it to re-appear in 15 seconds because it was isolated to the broom closet.

But the goldfish bowl did appear on the shelf from exactly where they had taken it, and no longer were just the two of them in the room; their exact doubles are also in the basement, doing and saying what they had just done.

They watched as Keith picked up one of the goldfish bowls and put it on the chair in the broom closet. They watched it all as if they were seeing an instant replay of a football game. When it came to the time that Keith hit the "enter" button, the other two men disappeared.

"Time for option two," Joe said humorously.

Keith laughed. "You've got to admit," he said," this is kind of fun. I was thinking, with all of the paranormal activity that people talk about, like ghost and spirits, that they are just people in a time machine. I mean, didn't you feel like you were a ghost?"

Amazed by what he had just witnessed Joe said, "I feel like a kid with a bicycle that I don't know how to ride. I was surprised by how light I felt. It was like I could just float around the room. Where do we go from here?"

Keith pondered that question for a moment and then said, "We go back ten yards and punt."

It had been two days since the last experiment with the time machine. Joe now knew he was not going to die or turn to dust by traveling back in time, as Keith suggested. He was running out of patience and did not want to spend years testing this thing before he could really do what he wanted to do. Keith was being too cautious, Joe decided.

Joe knew that the problem of containing the area, affected by the time machine, had not been resolved. Did the whole house go back in time when they used it before or was it just the work room? He really didn't know, but he was planning on going back to the 1940s. To play it safe, he decided to go to their old plumbing office building. It had been empty since they built the new warehouse. It was an old brick building, built around 1900, so it definitely existed during the war. It had an old walk-in safe in it that should contain the effect and the energy of this machine. The walls, floor, and ceiling were made of about twelve inches of heavy concrete. The door was made of concrete reinforced with steel. The locking mechanism had been removed, so that no one could accidentally be locked inside.

Joe decided to leave Keith a note, just in case something went wrong and he could not get back to the present. He left the notes on the chair in the workshop where he figured Keith would look for him. He explained what he planned to do and that he was going to the warehouse.

I feel like I'm leaving a suicide note, he thought to himself. *I'll be all right! There is always the "recall" button if I get into trouble. Joe reminded himself.*

At the old office building, Joe pondered what place he wanted to go to first. He decided to start with a date in 1941, when he was only two-days old, then he programmed in the address that he had been given from Naomi.

Joe programmed in "December 11th, 1941." He put in 20 minutes in the time lapse section to insure that he would not get stuck in that time era. He double checked the complete address, including the spelling on the screen, to make sure that he spelled the street name correctly. He certainly did not want to wind up at the wrong place at the wrong time.

Joe walked to the middle of the old office building. He steadfastly stepped into the old safe and closed the door. He realized that he was much more nervous than he had expected to be. His hands were physically shaking. He was actually sweating, the same way he did whenever he sat in a doctor's office, waiting to be examined. As unsure as he was, he was determined to overcome his fears by doing what he always did in situations of apprehension. He shouted, out loud, "Let's do it," as he pushed the "enter" button.

Immediately, he is transformed to a very warm, well-furnished and neat room decorated in the 1940s style. There appeared to be a stack of cut-up pictures on the coffee table. He recognized the woman talking on an old fashion, large, black, dial type telephone, as his mother. Of course she was much younger than he ever remembered her. She was just as beautiful and he desperately wanted to put his arms around her desperately and tell her that he loved her. Then he realized that she was crying. Joe heard her speak into the phone, "This poor, pathetic woman and her bastard son don't need your pity."

The words "bastard son" hit Joe in the face like a sudden cold spray of water from a garden hose. Joe knew that his mother and father were married. He had seen their marriage license which was dated at least a year before he was born. It seemed as if Joe's mother had hung up on whomever was on the other end of the phone. She picked up the pile of pictures from the coffee table and threw them in the garbage.

She obviously could not see Joe desperately and as he came near to console her, she walked right through him. She then walked into the bedroom and patted the little boy sleeping in the crib. With a tearful voice she whispered, "If Joseph was a good enough name for the man who raised Jesus, it is good enough for you."

She then lay down on the well-made bed and cried hysterically. As Joe watched his mother, he felt like crying himself because of the sorrow he knew she was feeling. *She must be crying over the death of her husband,* Joe assumed. *Why else? But something else is wrong.*

As suddenly as Joe had been transformed to his mother's apartment, he was now again back in the warehouse safe. He composed himself enough to look at his watch; it was the same time as when he pushed the "enter" button.

The time machine didn't matter to him at that moment. He had a broken heart from seeing his mother being so miserable, so devastated, so dejected. He needed to talk to Keith... Or should he? Maybe he should talk to Aunt Naomi... or maybe not. He would decide that the next day, but just then, he just needed to compose him self, after what he had seen.

Joe sat in almost total darkness with only a small lamplight in the living room glowing. He sat at the kitchen table, which he referred to as his thinking table, where he did his best thinking. He knew that Keith would be upset when he discovered what he had done. He dreaded telling him but he decided that the sooner he did, the better it would be. His motto had always been to do the things that he did not want to do, as fast as he could. That way, he would not create extra stress worrying about it. He needed to tell Keith and he planned to do it immediately.

Joe reached for the phone and hit Keith's speed dial number. After he blurted out his story, Joe got exactly the reaction from Keith that he expected.

"Okay," Joe said into the phone. "I knew you'd be mad and I don't blame you. But when you get done with your little rant, I need to tell you what happened. I need your advice as to what to do next. Can you come over tomorrow? I'm not at the lake; I'm here in Rock Island."

In a matter-of-fact tone, Keith said, "I'll be there in 15 minutes!"

Keith arrived right on time. He walked in the back door without knocking, flipped on the kitchen light, fixed himself a drink without speaking and sat across the table from Joe. Neither man spoke for a long time.

Finally, Joe said, "I guess you want to listen since you're not talking."

Joe gave Keith a step by step account of his latest adventure with the time machine.

"I think that the warehouse was a great idea." Keith said when he finally cooled down and decided to speak. "The fact that mom was upset doesn't surprise me. She just found out that her husband and the father of her baby was dead."

Unconvinced Joe said, "I suppose that you're right, but I just had this feeling that there was more to it than that. Why do you think that she tore up the pictures and threw them away? I mean, Mom always said that all of the pictures of my real dad were destroyed but she never said that she destroyed them... and what about the 'bastard child' thing...?"

In as much compassion as he could express, Keith said, "Joe, you are my brother and I only want what's good for you. Maybe you need to stop this now."

Abruptly Joe said, "Keep it down; Virginia is upstairs sewing and I don't want here to hear about this. She already thinks I am up to something. But I can't stop now. We need to ask Aunt Naomi some more things. I know that it wasn't a very good idea the last time we tried it, and it isn't any better an idea, now; but I need to try."

In response Keith stated, "If you won't leave the past in the past, there is only one thing to do. We need to go on another trip to somewhere we know your father will be. You've got the original marriage license. It tells you when and where they were married. That's a party you need to attend."

Joe agreed, "We go tomorrow morning."

"Great," agreed Keith. To break the tension, he said, "I always loved weddings. Do I need to wear a suit?"

CHAPTER EIGHT

The next morning the two men met at the warehouse, Joe had the marriage license with him and Keith programmed the time machine to just the right time and place.

"Are you ready to finally see what your dad looked like?" Keith asked Joe.

"Let's do it," Joe replied and hit the "enter" button.

The transformation from present time to the past was as instantaneous, as before. Joe and Keith are standing in the lobby of the San Diego City Hall on October 18, 1940. There was a handful of people bustling around. Joe looked around to see if he could find his mother, but he did not see her. Then he looked toward the front entrance and saw two sailors entering wearing their dress whites. One of the men looked to be Japanese. The other is a blond headed man about twenty years old.

"So that's where I got my blond hair from" Joe mused to himself. He always figured that he got his hair color from his dad because his mother's hair was brown.

The men were followed closely by two women, whom he immediately recognized as his mother and Aunt Naomi. Joe's breath was almost taken away by the beauty of the two women. His mother, so young, so trim and wearing a pure white dress that reached to the floor. It set off beautifully her shoulder length brown hair and her big brown eyes. Aunt Naomi was wearing a pink dress that fit her like a glove. He had often wondered how someone so beautiful could stay single all her life. She had never even dated a guy to the best of his knowledge.

As if watching a play, Joe observed the four as they walk straight to the reception desk. The Japanese man told the lady behind the desk that they were Cora Edwards and Jerry Adams and that they had come to get married. *He's got to be dad's best man,* Joe assumed.

"Are there two witnesses with you?" the clerk asked.

"Yes," the Japanese man answered. The clerk directed them to stand in the corner and told them that she would notify them when the judge was ready. As the four waited in the corner, Joe burned into his mind everything he could about this tall, blond headed man who was talking to Naomi. Joe's heart was filled with joy and excitement to be there and to witness this event. He finally had the chance to see, and study his father.

Then Joe heard the Japanese man say to his mother, "It would have been nice if this wedding could happen in a big church; but your family is on the West Coast and mine is in Hawaii."

Joe's confusion over that statement was interrupted by the court announcer hollering, "Adams and Edward follow me please."

Joe and Keith followed the four as they entered a small court room. At the end of the room in front of the large bench stood a man wearing a black robe; the four walked up to the man and he introduced himself as Judge Daniel McKee.

"Will the bride and groom please step forward, and hold hands. The witness may stand to the side of the bride and groom."

The Japanese man and Joe's mother, Cora walked to the Judge and with smiles on their faces, grasped each other's hands. Aunt Naomi positioned herself to the left of Joe's mother and the blond headed man moved to the right of the Japanese man.

There was a moment of nothingness in Joe's mind and soul. He just froze, unable to speak or even think. Suddenly he yelled out loud, "NO! You've got this all wrong."

Joe tried to grab the shoulder of the Judge but his hand went right through him.

"Dearly beloved, we are gathered here before me and these wetness." the Judge started to say.

Joe jumped between the Judge and his mother, but no one paid any attention to him.

"This thing must be broken" Joe yelled as he beat the time machine on his hand. Joe looked at Keith and hollered, "There must be something wrong with this thing. It's got things mixed up!"

Keith reached out his hand and took the time machine from Joe. He realized that there was nothing wrong with the machine and understood the shock that his brother was going through.

"There's nothing wrong with it," Keith spoke timidly.

Without saying a word, Keith pushed the "reset" button and the two shaken men were back in the warehouse.

The silence in the warehouse came from the lack of either man knowing what to say. They walked slowly to Joe's car, without saying a word. Keith still possessed the time machine. He patted Joe on the back without saying anything, and then walked to his own car. He waited for Joe to start his car and drive away. Keith followed him until Joe pulled into his own driveway, again. Keith then followed Joe into the house.

The two brothers sat opposite each other at Joe's kitchen table just staring into the drinks that Keith made for them. The room was illuminated only by the midday sun streaming in the windows. Keith wished it was night so that the room would be dark. Each man was consumed with his own thoughts, which in fact, were the same thoughts.

The silence was finally broken when Joe said, "I don't have an oriental bone in my body!"

"I know," said Keith, "and mom was definitely married to your dad when you were born."

"He's not my real dad!" Joe quickly responded. "My real dad is the best man. He has to be. You did something wrong when you built that machine."

"There is nothing wrong with that machine." Keith reassured Joe. "The only thing wrong is us thinking that we knew what the truth was. The father that you wanted to save on the Arizona, all those years, was not your father. You have figured that out just like I have. All the dreams you had were based on misinformation. The only option I see now is to go back and confront Aunt Naomi. She must have known the truth. I want to know the truth too. Your father may not have been my father, but your mother is mine. Our mother didn't lie and she certainly wouldn't cheat on her husband when he was away at sea."

"You're right," Joe reacted aggressively. "And this time it's not going to be us as little boys talking to our elder. We're going to get into the mud, the blood and the beer. Let's do it!"

CHAPTER NINE

Naomi greeted Joe and Keith at the front door. "Well, to what do I owe the pleasure of this visit, again so soon? Come in and join me for some tea," she said. "Make yourselves comfortable and I will get the tea."

The two men sat beside each other on the overstuffed davenport in the living room. Naomi returned from the kitchen with the tea. "Now, what is it that I can do for you on such a pretty day?" she asked.

"We know that Jerry Adams, the man who is supposed to be my father was Oriental. He couldn't possibly be my father," Joe announced to Naomi. "It's not a suspicion, Aunt Naomi; we know it for a fact" Joe continued. "And I've come to ask you what's going on. Who was my real father and how did that happen?"

Realizing that she could not avoid the question, and the secret she was hoping she would take with her to her grave, Naomi turned her face and attention to Keith. She was hoping, somehow, that she might avoid the situation, by changing the person to whom she was speaking.

"What is he talking about?" Naomi asked Keith. "Where did he get an idea like that?"

"Stop it, Aunt Naomi," Keith said harshly. "We know the truth. You were there when Mom married Jerry. We know that you helped Mom with the deception that made Joe think that Jerry Adams was his real father and that you know much more than you have ever said. You owe it to Joe, and you owe it to me, to tell us the whole truth."

Still trying to avoid the questions and stalling while she gathered her thoughts, Naomi asked "And just how do you know that?"

"It's not important how we know but believe me we do know that to be the truth," Keith said in a tone that Naomi understood meant the "gig was up".

Naomi considered her situation and said to Joe, "Okay, you're right. Jerry Adams wasn't your natural father. He was an asshole and you should be glad that he wasn't your father. He treated your mother like shit and if he hadn't died at Pearl Harbor, I'd probably have eventually killed him myself." With a more excited voice now, Naomi continued; "Your mother only wanted to protect you from the truth. What was she supposed to do? Her husband was dead. You needed to have a last name and she wanted you to grow up normally. Should she have given you her husband's name, her maiden name or someone else's name?"

Naomi's excitement level seemed to rise quickly as she talked. Her words became more intense as she uttered them as fast as she could. She said, "Jerry Adams is dead and good riddens but it just made sense for your mom to leave Jerry Adams' name as your father on the birth certificate."

"Who the hell is my father then?" Joe asked.

"How do I know," Naomi snapped back. "I will tell you this much, your mother was not unfaithful to her husband. She was brutally raped. Your mother didn't know who the man was. Her husband was dead, her son was born. She loved her husband and you, even more. So what was left for her to do, but to protect you? She did what she did, not for herself… but for you!"

Naomi sat back in her overstuffed chair, took a deep breath and a sip of tea. In a more relaxed tone said, "I will not betray your mother. I may not have agreed with her when she came up with that hair brain idea but it was her decision to make. I have supported her most of my life. I can't see how knowing, today, that Jerry Adams is not your real father has improved your life one little bit, over what you thought yesterday. There are many things in the past, that we are better off not knowing. Your mother never told me who the man was that sired you; the man who raped her wasn't your father. The great man that raised you was your father from the day he met you. Any man can make a baby, any man can abandon a baby but it takes a real man to raise a baby."

Joe pondered what she said for a moment, and then replied, "You may be right, Aunt Naomi, I may have been better off not knowing; but now that I do know, I can't let it go. I have to keep looking until I find the answers. Will you help me learn the whole truth?"

"I won't be disloyal to your mother's wishes." Naomi said. Naomi was absolutely certain that there is no possible way for Joe to learn the identity of his real father, or the circumstances surrounding his conception.

"As I told you already," Naomi said," your mother didn't know who your father was and that is the truth. Now you boys are digging in ground with no potatoes, so just give it up."

Joe believed her, but felt that she still knew more than she is willing to tell. There was more to the story that she was not sharing but he also realized that there was no point in pursuing her for more information. The two men thanked her for her help and kissed Aunt Naomi good-bye. As the two men walked to the car, Naomi hollered at them, from the front porch, "I could use a new bike for my birthday!"

"It looks like we're going to need to take some trips." Joe said to Keith.

"Yep," replied Keith. "But we need to figure out just where we're going from here."

"I want to find out who the best man at the wedding was," Joe said. "Right now he is my number one suspect."

"Come on Joe." Keith says doubtfully, "Don't you think that your mother would have recognized him as her rapist?"

"I don't know; maybe she didn't get a good look at the guy, maybe she was in shock, maybe it isn't him. I don't know but I want to find out."

Back at Joe's house, Keith asked to see the marriage license. Joe knew what Keith was thinking. As the two men looked at the witness names on the license, they saw a name that was written in almost unreadable scribble. But they both agreed that the name was James Fleming.

"Well," Joe offered, "he could be either German or Irish, but he certainly wasn't Japanese. He had to be a good friend of Jerry's, if he was his best man. Do you think that he could have been at Pearl Harbor on the Arizona with him?"

"Could be," Keith concurred. "One thing that we do know is that Jerry was stationed in San Diego, when he and our mother were married, and that he was assigned to the Arizona a couple of months before you were born. This James Fleming could have been sent there too. We can check the names of the men who were on the Arizona, on the internet, and see what we find."

They were right. James Fleming was stationed on the Arizona but his name was not on the list of the men who died there. Just to be sure, the men double checked the list of those who lost their lives when the U.S.S. Arizona was sunk that day.

"Do you notice anything strange about the list," Keith questioned Joe.

"Yes," Joe said softly. "Jerry Adams' name isn't on this list of those who died either."

Keith looked up at Joe and asked, "Is it possible that James Fleming is still alive? Maybe the two men were on shore leave and didn't get back before the attack. Maybe they weren't on the ship and they didn't die that day. It would be impossible for our mother to have cheated on her husband. There has to be a rational explanation for this whole thing. The questions kept coming. If the two men didn't die that day, what happened to them?"

"We need to find out more about James Fleming and the best place to start would be for us to go back to the Arizona." Keith stated, "December 7th, 1941, was a Sunday. The Arizona was in port and it was peace time. Most of the crew would be on shore leave. Typically, weekend passes in peace time started at 1600 hours on Fridays. So if we went back to the Friday evening before, and followed Jerry and James, we might get some answers."

CHAPTER TEN

Keith set the time machine for December 5th, 1941. He typed in Pearl Harbor, Hawaii, 4:00 PM.

"I'm not sure what time I should place us there because I don't know exactly when they would go on shore leave or if they would have already gone," he told Joe. "It's just a guess."

Without a moment of hesitation, Joe repeated his favorite words, "Sounds good to me. Let's do it!"

Keith pushed the "enter" button. Joe and Keith were instantly transported to the naval base on the island of Oahu, Hawaii, known as Pearl Harbor. They made their way to the gang plank of the Arizona.

"If they're still on board and they go on shore leave, we might be able to spot them, if we stand here." Keith told Joe.

They watched for a couple of hours while sailors came and went, carefully checking each one.

"Look," Joe finally said. "Isn't that them coming, now?"

They followed the two sailors as they hailed a cab. Joe and Keith slipped inside the cab with the two men.

"Streamer's Restaurant in Pismo Beach," Jerry told the driver.

"Are you going over to see your mother?" James asked Jerry.

"Yea, I thought we'd have a few drinks at Streamer's and then I need to go see her."

"That's fine. I'm going to do a little skirt chasing later, and I know you're not into that. I'll see you later," James said.

Joe and Keith hadn't considered that the men might split up. They quickly agreed that Keith would follow Jerry, and Joe would follow

James. The only trouble was that they only had the one time machine. They agree that Joe would keep the time machine. Jerry was the first to leave the restaurant with Keith following.

Joe stayed behind and watched James continue to get drunk. What happened next was so shocking that Joe pushed the return button early. Suddenly, the two brothers were again back in the warehouse. The look on Joe's face told Keith that he had been through something terrible.

"What in the world is the matter with you?" Keith asked Joe.

"He raped my mother!" Joe screamed.

"What are you talking about?" Keith insisted.

"I watched him. I saw him try to rape a different girl and I know that he did the same thing to our mother, months before when they were stateside. It all makes perfect sense," Joe said.

Keith tried to calm Joe down as they drove back to Joe's house. Joe described to Keith how he watched James for hours, drink and drink. The more he drank, the nastier he got with the waitresses. When three Marines came in, James smarted off to them when they told him to leave the waitresses alone. A crashing blow from this gorilla in a Marine uniform put James on his back. They violently threw him out of the bar and out into the street. He told Keith that he watched as James stumbled into an alley, more drunk then hurt. As he lay there bleeding and moaning, a young lady, walked by, saw a hurt man and went into the alley to help him.

Joe excitedly went on to describe how he watched as James beat the hell out of the defenseless girl. "He had his hand on her throat so she couldn't yell. He tore off her clothes with his free hand, but she managed to break loose of his strangle hold long enough to scream. The Shore Patrol must have been fairly close by, because they came running down the alley and clubbed him with their night sticks until he was out cold."

"What?" Keith said in complete disbelief.

"James was so drunk and so intense in what he was doing that he didn't even hear them coming. I heard one of the Shore Patrol sailors say to the other that he must be the guy who had been attacking all of the women lately. It all made sense. It all made perfect sense now, with Mom."

Keith's eyebrows were raised. His mouth fell open with a look of total revelation. "Now that you mention it, he did look a lot like you." Keith finally managed to say.

"You're right. That would answer a lot of questions. If he was a serial rapist, and if he was in the brig, that would explain why he didn't die on the Arizona too."

Keith completely forgot the journey that he had been on. His thoughts were fully concentrated on his and Joe's sorrow, for the hurt and suffering that their mother endured. Knowing her as they did, they understood that she would do everything to protect her child.

"That was just like her," Joe said. "It is a shame that we didn't realize how really great she was while she was alive." He never thought that he could love his mother more than he did when she was alive; but at that moment, he began to understand her more completely. His love grew to more than love. There was also deep admiration for her, as a survivor.

Then a thought crossed his mind. *"If James was the best man at her wedding, why wouldn't she recognize him as her attacker? Maybe she did but couldn't bring herself to bring more shame to her husband by revealing that to him."*

The next day was Saturday, Joe and Keith knew enough about Naomi to realize that she would be at the mall, shopping until about noon. Then she often went to The Village Inn Restaurant with her girlfriends for lunch. She would probably be home around one thirty. They made plans to go over to talk to her around two.

Joe questioned Keith about the wisdom of telling Aunt Naomi what they found out and wondered out loud what that would accomplish. And might she begin to question how they knew all of these facts?

"She knew more than she was telling us," Keith began. "She said that mom didn't tell her who your father really was but I got the feeling she always had an idea of who it was. She may be willing to tell us more now, that we know that mom was raped."

"What more can she add?" Joe asked.

"I don't know but I just feel there's more! Did she know that Jerry didn't die on the Arizona and does she know what happened to him?"

"Oh!" Keith blurt out. "I haven't had a chance to tell you what I learned when I followed Jerry."

Keith told Joe that Jerry did indeed go to his mother's house or at least he believed it was her house. When they went in, the house was full of people, mostly Japanese. But there was some English being spoken. It was broken English with Japanese words mixed in, but Keith heard enough to get an idea of what was happening at the meeting.

"There was talk of the messages that they had been sending to Japan. There was some talk about the attack that was coming. They didn't seem to know exactly when it was coming but they were told to get out of town."

Keith told Joe that they left the home and immediately went to the airport and boarded a plane headed for Japan.

"What? Are you telling me that Jerry Adams was a Japanese spy?" Joe asked incredulously.

"That's exactly what I'm telling you," Keith answered back.

Keith continued his story and told Joe how he followed the group onto the airplane, and stated that the people who spoke to Jerry on the plane, talked to him in Japanese but a few conversed with him in English.

Keith finished his story by saying, "They didn't call him Jerry Adams, and they called him Takeo Yosohikawa."

Puzzled by his last comment, Joe asked, "So what difference does it matter, what they called him?"

Keith realized that Joe did not understand, or know the name of the person, he had just told him.

"I've been doing a lot of studying on Pearl Harbor," He continued. "Takeo Yosohikawa and his mother were the leaders of a spy ring in Hawaii. The Japanese had planned to attack Pearl Harbor for a long time. The man you thought was your father and his mother had been sending messages to Japan about the naval fleet. They told them everything they needed to know for the attack."

"Whatever happened to him?" Joe asked.

"Jerry Adams was a double agent who was working for both the American and Japanese sides during the war."

Keith told Joe that Jerry was acting as a spy for the Japanese so that he could give information to the Americans. Although he knew that the Japanese had planned an attack somewhere in the Pacific, he didn't expect it to be Hawaii particularly without them declaring war first.

"The Japanese were a very proud people who considered honor to be a greater value then life," Keith explained. "Samurai who were going to attack someone who was sleeping would wake them and hand them a sword first. To do anything less would be considered disgraceful. Even though Jerry was taken by surprise, by the attack on Pearl Harbor, many Japanese were convinced that he was part of the dishonorable act and shunned him for the rest of his life. He died, penniless, a disgraced old man in a nursing home in Japan after the war."

"And what about his mother; what happened to her?" asked Joe.

"She was killed when we dropped the atomic bomb on Nagasaki," Keith told him.

"Couldn't happen to a better person," Joe said sarcastically.

Joe and Keith arrived at Naomi's house at exactly two o'clock fearing that if they got there any later she would be gone to a poker game or some other crazy event that this eccentric woman did. They rang the doorbell, and sure enough, when she opened the door, she was wearing her karate outfit.

"Aunt Naomi," Joe said. "Can we come in and talk? It's important!"

"I'm running kind of late," was her response.

"We know mom was raped," Keith jumped in. "And we know who did it."

Without missing a beat, almost as if she was expecting them she said, "Well then, I guess you better come in."

As the three walked the short distance from the front door to the living room, thoughts ran thru Naomi's mind in an instant. *How could they know?* She wondered. She remembered the first time she saw little Joe, the overwhelming bond that she seemed to have for him. She had been around many babies and never felt the way she did when she first saw him.

She knew, at her brother's funeral, what that look in Cora's eyes was all about. She saw the horror, the shame and knew what Cora was thinking. Naomi didn't know how or why, but she knew that her brother had raped Cora. She had always tried to deny it to herself, but it was there in Cora's eyes. She knew that Cora had never met her brother. Whenever she was at Naomi's mother's house, where she and her brother lived, her brother was busy doing something else and it was just too coincidental that he was never around. And when she was moving in with Cora, her brother happily helped her pack, loaded her car with her things, but would not go over to Cora's home to help unload. Why not? It had to be, the blue eyes, the blond hair and the resemblance. It had to be true. And now Joe and Keith had figured it out!

As they entered the living room, Joe told Naomi, "A man named James Fleming raped mom. Remember him?" Joe asked. "He was Jerry's best man at mom and Jerry's wedding. You must have known him."

Naomi did not get shocked by many things, but what she had just heard was an exception. Slowly she sat down in her usual chair while the two men positioned themselves on the davenport.

Naomi regained her wits. "No, I didn't know him. I talked to him, a little, at city hall, but I really didn't pay much attention to him. I had never seen him before that day or since. Jerry mentioned him often but your mother and I had never met him before. I was so involved with your mother, the wedding and all; that I just didn't pay much attention to him."

Joe and Keith shared everything that they had learned, although they didn't tell Naomi about the time machine. They told her about James getting caught in the act trying to rape another girl in Hawaii. They told her how he lured the girl into an alley by pretending he was hurt.

"Your mom and I were both nurses. If she came across someone in trouble and in need of medical care, it wouldn't matter if it was in a hog lot, she'd go to help." Naomi declared with her strong Texan accent that came out more when she was upset.

"Yes, I knew she'd been raped. I knew she didn't want her baby to be a result of that terrible incident, and truly wanted it to be Jerry's baby. I know how Jerry treated her after he found out. Ya! I knew lots of things, but it was your mom who protected you all those years. It was none of your business to know things then, and it still ain't. You smart ass boys need to honor your mothers wishes and leave the past alone. There ain't nothing you're goanna do to change what is! It doesn't matter if your dad was a long horn bull, you're still what you are and there is nothing wrong with that. I don't know who the hell you guys think you are, but I can tell you that you need to leave well enough alone."

"We love you, Aunt Naomi, and we understand how you feel," Keith tried to smooth over the situation. "We don't love mom, or you, any less. In fact, we probably love her more now that we know. But we are going to keep searching for the truth. And I think you also would like to know some things. Let's work together to get the true facts."

Naomi asked that the boys excuse her for a minute. "I think that I have a picture of the wedding that your mother didn't know I had kept. I want to see if we are talking about the same person."

Naomi returned with a large box and began going through it as the boys looked over her shoulder.

"Here it is." she said as she held it up for Joe to see. "Is this the man you are talking about?" she asked as she pointed at a man in a picture with her, Jerry, and their mother.

The two sailors were dressed in their whites and the two women were dressed just as Joe and Keith had seen them, when they went back and observed the marriage.

"If you didn't really know him very well," Joe questioned, "then why do you have an 8x10 picture of him?"

As the three looked closer at the box, they saw the very next picture in the pile was a large picture of the same man. Naomi's mouth fell wide open for a moment then she said, "No, that's my brother!"

"You're telling us that those two pictures are not of the same person?" Keith asked.

Naomi lifted the picture of her brother from the box and turned it over. His name followed by 1942, are handwritten on the back of the picture. When she turned it back over to the front again, the three saw the photographer's symbol, in the lower corner of the picture, with the date 1942.

"I wouldn't have believed that these were two different men, but I don't think they allow someone to have a cameo done while they are in the brig."

Keith asked Naomi how she could not have ever noticed the resemblance before. She had never seen her brother in a sailor suit and the two men were built a lot differently.

"I don't know. I just didn't see it till now."

Now she understood that look in Cora's eyes, at her brother's funeral. She died thinking that it was her brother who raped her. Naomi was filled with the feeling of both extreme happiness and heartbreak, at the same time. She could never understand how her wonderful brother could possibly do such a terrible thing, and she was jubilant over the idea that he hadn't. But she felt heartbroken over the thought that Cora had gone through the pain she did, in order to protect the people she loved. Cora's painful secret must have been overwhelming, at times. However, the love she possessed was greater than the pain and suffering she endured throughout her lifetime. That was what always won out for her.

"I've got to tell you about what we learned about Jerry," Joe interrupted Naomi's thoughts.

Joe told Naomi that Jerry was not on the Arizona, but instead, he was on a plane headed for Japan when the attack happened. He told her what he knew about Jerry being a spy, his real name, and the way that he died.

"You're telling me that you've been obsessed about a father, who wasn't your father, who died on the Arizona as a war hero, when he wasn't even there and your dreams for years about finding a way to go back and save his life? I think I know frogs smarter than you," she said.

A feeling of frustration began to rise in Joe's body. Through this whole adventure, he had not felt that he was being foolish, and now to have her suggest such a thing made him almost agree with her. Never in his life had he ever been angry with Aunt Naomi, or his mother, but suddenly he wondered if their deceit would change his feelings.

"Looking back, it may seem that I am dumber than a frog. But my life was based on lies. As well intentioned as those lies were, they were still lies. My mother tried to protect me from what she saw as a horrible burden for me. I love her for her sacrifice, and honor you for your loyalty to her, but for you to call me stupid for wanting to know the truth, seems hypocritical to me.

For the first time in his life, he saw embarrassment on her face. He wished that he could take back his outburst and just had ignored what she had said.

"Do you know what ever happened to James Fleming, your real father?" Naomi asked, not responding to what he had said.

Keith had researched this and told her. "James Fleming was tried by a military court because he was in uniform when he attempted to rape that girl in the alley. At trial, he was identified by five other women whom he had raped. He had been raping women for a long time. He also was suspected of raping many women in San Diego while he was stationed there. He was found guilty of all charges and executed by the military in accordance to military justice."

The two men came to Naomi's house wondering how much she knew, and if she was hiding the identity of their mother's rapist from them. They both realized when they left her home, that although she did know that their mother had been raped, she really didn't know who did it. She may have thought that she knew but she didn't. They realized that although she didn't tell them all she knew, she didn't exactly lie to them, either. She just didn't tell the whole truth and she arranged her words so that she didn't tell them things that she felt would be a betrayal to their mother. They didn't feel that she was right in the way she handled things, but they accepted that she did what she thought was best. Besides, how could a person, not love an eighty-year-old woman who sat across from them; having a serious conversation, while wearing karate outfit?

CHAPTER ELEVEN

As Joe sat on his front deck, at the lake, in the dark, watching the moon's reflection on the water; he looked up into the sky and marveled at the blanket of stars which could only be seen and appreciated, in the absences of city lights. He was feeling very lonely and wished that his wife had been able to come up, but she had to watch the grandson's baseball game. The radio was playing soft music inside the house. He loved sitting in the dark, looking up at the stars in the sky, feeling the calm breeze and listening to the sounds of the night. The music from the radio was interrupted by a special alert about a missing child and an Amber Alert that has been posted. He only half heard it. He was reflecting on all that had happened. *I kind of wish that I never started this, nothing has changed, my mother still went through what she went through; my life hasn't changed at all, not that I wanted it too. What's the point? Knowing the truth about the past doesn't help the present at all. It just seems to complicate things. Aunt Naomi was right, let the past rest in peace. Maybe the world would be better off, if I just dropped this thing in the lake.*

Without any warning, he had that indescribable feeling like static electricity covering his body. Suddenly he was transported to a large room that appeared to be a lawyer's office; a room that, once he got there, he remembered well. He looked toward the fireplace, saw the person standing there and knew exactly where he was. He remembered being there before and he recalled everything that had happened since the last time.

With apprehension, he walked to the easy chair in front of the fire and waited to hear what would occur. In that same baritone voice, Dr. Webster thoughts entered Joe's mind.

"Hello Joe."

Joe hadn't remembered anything about the experience of being on the ship or Dr. Webster once he was sent back to earth, but in this setting, he remembered it all.

Why, he wondered, *would I be here a second time?*

Reading Joe's thoughts, Dr. Webster said to Joe, without speaking and in a manner that made Joe think of a computerized voice. W*e will get to that in a few minutes. Please, make yourself comfortable and tell me; how was your experience?*

I wish he would stop doing that, Joe reasoned to himself. I*t's just not right to talk without speaking; it's spooky.*

Sorry, Joe, Dr. Webster replied, *but as you remember I am unable to speak. Besides, remember all of the other advantages to mind communication that we talked about the last time you were here. Language is not a problem that we need to overcome. I can communicate with you in my form of speech; and in your mind, you hear what I am thinking, in your language. There are no misunderstandings this way, and you tell me things that you don't realize you are thinking. For example, you were just thinking that you would prefer to be talking to my receptionist, Marilyn, rather than me. That's okay, Joe. My feelings are not injured and you do find her very attractive."*

"Have you been following me?" Joe asked.

I must confess that we did assign an agent to monitor your movements, Dr. Webster explained. *This was, for us, an experiment to see how you humans would handle the advance technology of time travel in your present state of evolution. I noted that you are wondering if we are human or extra-terrestrial beings. I would like to assure you that yes, we are actually human but so much more advanced than you, in your mind, that we don't consider you fully human. In fact, we have bred with people from your planet and watched the results of that offspring, but I digress. There is so much more that could be done with a time machine than what you have done.* He told Joe. *The planet that I come from is twenty million light years away from the earth. We use time manipulation combined with magnetism and motion to overcome that distance. You could assist with your Earth's space program which will remain limited in its usefulness until they understand how to use time to their advantage. You could use the time machine to keep from getting any older; there are an unlimited number of things that time manipulation is used for. You however are disappointed in the results that you achieved in your first interactions with the past. It has come to my attention that you are considering destroying the machine along with the plans you drew. You are having serious regrets about building the crude devise that your brother assembled.*

Joe said out loud, "You told me that it was possible to change the past, but you can't. You can only see the past the way it actually happened. I couldn't stop the bombing of Pearl Harbor. I could only watch it happen. And there is no way that I could stop the rape of my mother."

Many good things can come from painful experiences, Dr. Webster preached. *After your mother first laid eyes on you, and after raising you, given the choice between you and being raped, I think that she would pick you and your family. And whether you recognize it or not, you did change history. A few days ago you, your brother and Naomi discovered the whole truth. A few days ago are now history and it was changed. Even if you don't want the things you three have learned to change anything, it has to change the future. The knowledge you gained from the past has changed the three of you permanently. Those changes may be good or bad. Only the future will tell.*

Joe considered what Dr. Webster had just explained and realized that he needed to take some time to digest it and better understand his point.

Now it's time to address the reason we summoned you, Dr. Webster said. *We feel that, after watching you, your planet has not evolved enough. Some of your species would use time motion at this time for undesirable purposes. You have not discovered how to change the past, but I assure you it can be done. We also realize that you are having internal conflict over the positives and the negatives, of the knowledge that you and others, now have. So, for those and other reasons, we have decided to discontinue this experiment. You will be sent back to the moment before you came to visit us the first time with no memory of the things that have happened.*

"Wait," Joe hollered out loud. "You haven't given us enough credit. Sure; things may have not worked out the way we had hoped the first time, but Thomas Edison wasn't successful either, on his first attempts. He thought DC voltage was the way to light cities. He was wrong. It took Nikola Tesla and AC voltage to get the job done."

Joe realized that he was not ready to give up yet. He and Keith had learned a lot. There was a lot more to learn and he wanted to be a part of something he knew someday would be of great value to mankind. He needed to think as fast as he could and talk just as fast.

"I know that others have been here before me. I know that they had problems at first, too. My son fell off his bicycle the first time he got on it, but now he rides motorcycles in competitions. Keith and I are willing to continue, so please don't give up on us so easily."

I am unaware of any further plans that you or your brother have in regards to time travel, Mr. Adams. My decision whether or not to end this experiment is predicated on your communicating to me what those plans are. If I could see any altruistic value or an affirmative result in your quest, I have authority to re-evaluate the state of affairs. Otherwise, I am sorry but I must terminate it now.

Joe was frantic. Yes, he had considered pitching the machine into the lake; but at that moment, faced with the prospect of losing it permanently, he was in a panic. No, he and Keith had not talked about any future plans, but he knew they both wanted to continue going back in time. There had to be many positive things that could come from having the ability to revisit the past, but at that moment, he could not think of even one. Dr. Webster explained that there were hundreds of things that the manipulation of time could be used for, but what? Joe needed to come up with something right then. It needed to be something that would change Dr. Webster's mind and Joe did not have any time to waste. Suddenly, it came to him.

"We could use it to find missing children and save them from terrible things happening to them," he blurted out.

Interesting idea, Dr. Webster communicated. *I am surprised that you came up with something so positive in such a short time. It could be used to protect children from harm or let the authorities know what has happened to them.*

As quickly as he could respond, Joe said, "Yes, and if we used it right, we might be able to stop crime completely. Would a bad guy commit a crime, any crime, if he knew that he could be seen doing it?"

No, he would not, agreed Dr. Webster. *Your planet does have a large crime problem. Your court systems are overburdened and your prisons are filled to capacity. If done correctly, you could eliminate much crime. And the suggested concept about protecting and finding lost children is an excellent idea.*

The tension eased for Joe. He was not sure where he came up with the idea of finding missing children. Perhaps he subconsciously remembered the Amber alert that he had heard on TV. He didn't think that he had really listened to it. It always hurt too much to think of a child who was missing. Way too many times it was followed with the death of the child, or they were never found.

"So, you'll give us another shot?" Joe asked confidently, believing that he had convinced Dr. Webster. He knew that he had. Not only did he hear a tone of approval in his words, but he thought that he might have even seen a twinkle in the eye of the always serious Dr. Webster.

You have surprised me, Mr. Adams! Dr. Webster inflected his words sheepishly. *It is very seldom that I change my mind about anything. I am not sure that you are capable of being victorious in mastering the skills necessary to accomplish the task you suggested. If I decide to permit you to proceed, it will be like last time. You will leave here with no memory of ever having been here. The only exception to your leaving unaware of your visit is that I will instill a deep desire to find missing, exploited and harmed children.*

CHAPTER TWELVE

Joe sat on the front deck, of their lake cabin, in the dark; he was watching the moon's reflection on the lake. The music from the radio was playing softly inside the house. He loved sitting in the dark, looking at the stars in the sky, the calm breeze, and listening to the sounds of the night. The music from the radio was interrupted by an announcement of a missing child and an Amber Alert was posted. Joe only half heard it, he was deep in thought about all that had happened. He mused to himself, *I kind of wish that I never started this.* Without warning, he had a feeling like static electricity overcome his body. This was the same feeling that he had felt before. It was not normal. He had ignored it the last time it happened. He wondered if something was going on with his health. It had been a while since he been to the doctor for a physical. Maybe it was time to have a check-up.

Then he heard the repeated announcement on the radio, "...eight year old Carol Bridges was abducted from the alley behind her home, in the 44 hundred block of 9th Avenue. Witnesses claim they saw her being pulled into a late model green Chevrolet at about five forty five. The report said that she had brown hair and brown eyes. She was four foot five inches tall. She was wearing a white top and blue short. Anyone with any information was being asked to call the nearest law enforcement agency."

A cold sweat came over Joe, as he heard the announcement. The thought of any child being lost, missing, or abducted was so painful that he seldom listened to the reports. There was nothing that he could do about it. The end results were seldom good. The thought of a child being so scared, so helpless, being beaten, raped and or murdered was just more than he could handle. It would be different if he could help them in some way, or at least do something to bring the perpetrator who harmed them, to justice. Joe wondered, *over the years, how many kids had been lost or abducted and never heard from again?* He knew that the police routinely did everything they could by following up on leads. The public formed search groups and walked the area where the child was last seen; they held prayer vigils and did what they could to comfort the parents, and family. But as time went by, in far too many cases, the trail grew cold and they were forgotten. With no witnesses, no clue, all that was left was questions.

Is this to be one more of those terrible stories? He considered as he listened more intently. *Where is she? Who took her, and why? Is she still alive right now? Perhaps she is, and just maybe whoever took her, hasn't harmed her yet. If the police knew where she was, possibly they could still save her.*

Joe reasoned that the police just needed to know who took her. His imagination was running so wild with ideas, that he had trouble keeping up with it. If he could use the time machine, he could go back in time to the moment she was taken. At least he could probably tell the police who had her. Conceivably, he could follow the person who took her and find out where they were. It is plausible that he could give the police enough information to help them get to the girl before something bad happened. But if he did, why would the police believe him? They would want to know how he knew where she was. How could he tell them? What would they think? He would figure the details out later, because just then, he knew what he had to do. There wasn't any time to spare; he did not have time to even talk to Keith. He had to do this immediately, if he was going to save the little girl. It might already be too late… but perhaps not.

Without a second thought, Joe grabbed the time remote from the kitchen table and ran to his car. He needed to get to the warehouse in Rock Island and back into the safe as quickly as he could. He knew what he must do, yet he did not know how to do it. He understood that he could not stop the abduction; he would be nothing more than a ghost watching the events as they unfold. What was he going to do if he saw the person trying to rape the little girl, or kill her? He worried that the sight of such a thing would not be something that he could live with. He was just a plumber. He was not trained for this type of situation. He prided himself on being strong, but he knew that he really was not, when it came to things like that.

"I just need to find out who took her and turn that information over to the police" he whispered to himself, under his breath.

As his car pulled up to the old warehouse, he had no answers. He just had a passion to help this little girl and he knew she was still alive. She just has to be. He just knew it. *God, let it be so, he prayed.*

Joe closed the door to the safe. The single light bulb hanging from the ceiling gave the whole room a feeling of total isolation and loneliness. It seemed to suggest to him that he was acting like a fool. Maybe he should reconsider his actions or at least wait to talk to Keith about it.

"NO!" He shouted to himself out loud. "I know what has to be done. There is no one else to save her and there's no time to waste."

He put in the address he heard on the radio and the time the witness said they saw the abduction. His whole body was shaking with the tension of the moment. He had real uncertainty about getting involved in this, but something drove him to move forward.

"Let's do this!" he hollered and pushed the 'enter' button.

Immediately, Joe was standing on the corner of 44th Street and 9th Avenue. He had set the time at exactly five forty-five, the time the witness said she saw the little girl being abducted. It was a quiet, residential neighborhood away from any heavy street traffic. There were only a few cars parked on the street. Most of these people parked their cars in their garages. He noticed a green Chevrolet sedan parked on the north side of the street, but other than that, the street was mostly empty of cars. The yards were neatly manicured. The style and construction of the homes indicated that this was an older neighborhood, built around the 1920s. Most of the residents were probably retired and had paid off their homes years ago. Joe wondered if the little girl was abducted while visiting her grandparents.

The radio said that the girl was abducted in the alley in the 44 hundred block of 9th Avenue, but was it the alley to the north or the south of 44th street? As he stood there trying to decide which way to go, he noticed an elderly woman run up to a house in the middle of the block of 9th Avenue. She was banging on the front door of the house and yelling at the top of her lungs. Joe knew what she was upset about and realized that he got there too late to see anything. He should have known that the time stated on the radio was an estimated time and that he should have allowed for that. He needed to get there earlier, but at least he knew in which alley the girl was abducted. He needed to recalculate and do it in a hurry. He pushed the "reset" button and was back in the warehouse.

As Joe stood in the warehouse safe again, he reset the time on the remote to five thirty, and started to wonder about the green Chevrolet that he noticed parked in front of the house where the old lady ran, so excitedly. It was the same make and color of the car described in the report, indicating it was involved in the abduction. But how could that be? It was parked there at five forty-five so it couldn't have been involved. Was there another green Chevrolet in that alley? Was this just a coincidence or were the police looking for the wrong vehicle? In her state of excitement, the elderly woman might have seen the green Chevy parked in front of the house and gotten confused. He should know in a few minutes.

"Let's do it," he repeated to himself and pushed the 'enter' button.

Again, he was standing on the corner of 44th Street and 9th Avenue. He moved in the direction of the green Chevrolet and noticed white lettering on the door of the car. As he got closer, he saw "Rock Island Township Assessor" printed in big bold letters on the car along with a phone number. *Interesting*, he noted. *I wonder how the elderly lady could have missed that.* He moved along the side of the house toward the alley. It was a brick, one-and-a-half story, well-maintained, older home with an enclosed front porch. Four steps lead up to the front door. To the right of the steps were four large numbers neatly fastened to the house that read, "4412." He noticed a two-car brick garage which was built on the alley and through the window; he could see that the garage door was open. He walked along side of the garage and stood in the alley.

The alley was paved with concrete and was in better shape than most streets were in the city. Each house on the block had its own garage; some had space for two cars, but most were single car garages. They were all set back from the alley at exactly the same distance. All of the garage doors were closed except for the one by which he was standing. Inside, on one side, was parked an older model, white Oldsmobile. On the other side was an empty space. There were no cars parked in the driveways along the alley, suggesting that these people did use their garages for their intended purposes. Other than the sound of a lawn mower humming in the distance, everything was as quiet as a graveyard.

From the end of the alley, he caught sight of a young girl who just turned the corner and was walking his direction. She looked to be about eight years old, and was just coming home from school. She was wearing a white, short sleeved blouse and blue shorts. As she walked closer, Joe noticed that she wore ear phones and was talking on a cell phone. Joe watched her every move, as the girl walked up the alley and was directly in front of him. Then she stopped and looked up the alley. Joe turned to see a blue Toyota coming down the alley from the opposite direction. The girl seemed to recognize the car and stopped walking until it drove up beside her.

From inside of the Toyota, Joe heard the voice of a man say, "Hi, Carol; how are you today?"

The young girl seemed to tense up but acknowledged the person in the car. The man stepped out of the car, walked around to the passenger side next to the rear door. He looked to be about 25 years old, approximately five feet ten inches tall and had a medium build. The black tee shirt he was wearing had a large Harley Davidson logo that covered the entire back. His blue jeans were faded and torn. They matched perfectly his dirty and worn out tennis shoes.

"Your mom wanted me to pick you up and take you home. She said she's twisted her ankle and needs you."

Carol's eyebrows raised in a look of surprise. She took a step back away from the man and her whole body seemed to tighten even more.

"I was just talking to her on the cell," Carol responded. "I mean, like, I just got off the phone with her. She didn't say anything like that."

The man's face turned instantly red. "JUST GET IN THE CAR," he screamed at Carol.

"I'M NOT GOING ANYWHERE WITH YOU," she hollered back.

Quick as a cat, almost as if practiced, the man pulled something small out of his back pocket and hit Carol in the temple. She fell to the ground instantly. The cell phone, on which she had been talking, fell from her hand and landed under the car. The man opened the rear door to the car, picked up Carol's small, limp body and stuffed her into the back seat. He ran back to the driver's side of the car, jumped in, and sped away down the alley. At the end of the alley, he did not stop for traffic but made a hard left turn. His tires squealed as he accelerated north onto 45th Street.

Frozen in shock at what he had just seen, Joe just stood motionless like one of the telephone poles lining the alley. When he finally began to regain his thoughts, he was trembling. His heart was pounding so hard he could hear it beating through his chest. He looked around hoping to see someone, anyone, who might help, but the alley was as empty of people as a cemetery is at night. The only sound was that lawn mower humming in the distance. He looked down at the remote in his hand and placed his thumb on the "reset" button when he heard a door slam. Just before he pushed the enter button, he caught sight of the elderly woman running wildly across the front yard to the brick house.

Back in the warehouse, Joe was angry with him self for not doing anything and for not being better prepared for what he knew was coming. He froze. He panicked, and he could not believe that he had reacted that way. He knew there was little that he could do but he could have gotten into the car with them and found out where the man had taken her. Why didn't he at least get the license number of the car? He wondered if he should do it again, should he go back a third time? The next time he would be prepared. But what good would it really do? He couldn't stop what had happened and time was wasting. She might still be alive and hopefully, reasonably well. He needed to get someone involved who could do something. He needed to contact the police.

CHAPTER THIRTEEN

Joe hurried from the warehouse safe back to his car, with only one thought on his mind. He knew exactly what to do, and where to go. But as he sat behind the steering wheel of his car, he was totally unsure of anything. How would he explain to the police how he knew what really happened? They would never believe that he had a way of going back in time and witnessing the abduction. They might even think that he was the one who took little Carol, or that he, at least, was a part of the plan to abduct her. He decided that he needed to calm down, clear his mind, and get his blood pressure under control. He needed to go home and have a drink. Rather than drive all the way back up to the lake, Joe decided to go to the Rock Island house. Whatever he was going to do, he knew time would be important and he didn't want to waste time driving.

As he sat in the den contemplating what to do, the clock on the wall began to chime. The usually sweet mild tone was seldom heard because he was so used to it; but right then, it seemed like it was nagging at him. He looked up at it and noted that it was nine o'clock. It was probable that a little girl's life was in his hands and if he did not do something pretty soon.... Joe finished his drink and picked up the phone. Joe had never called that number before. He had never had a need to dial it before, but he knew it well, as everybody did, just three little numbers, 911.

He heard only one ring on the other end when a woman answered and said in a tone of absolute authority, "Rock Island Police Department. What is your emergency?"

"I need to talk to someone about the Carol Bridges abduction"

"What is your name?" the almost rude woman asked.

Joe was surprised by that question because he knew that the Police Department had caller ID, he was calling from his home phone in Rock Island, and so she already knew who he was and where he was calling from. Then he rationalized that anyone could be calling the police from his phone.

"Joe Adams" he responded obediently.

"One moment please," he heard her say in what was a much more pleasant voice.

In less than a minute, another woman answered saying, "Hello, this is Detective Judy Martin. May I help you?"

In that instant Joe realized more fully the gravity of the situation. He was on the phone, talking to the police. How was he going to tell them what he knew, without them thinking he had something to do with it? But he knew that he had to say something.

"My name is Joe Adams. I live in Rock Island. I saw little Carol being kidnapped."

"And just what did you see?" the Detective asked in a tone that surprised Joe. In her calmness, she continued "If you don't really know anything, please don't waste our time, sir."

Joe realized from her tone that he needed to convince her that he was not just a prank call. He needed to make her take him seriously.

"I'm sure that you found little Carol's cell phone in the alley. I know that you didn't report that on the news release. I know that she had been talking to her mother on that cell phone just moments before she was abducted. I know that you are searching for the wrong make and color of the car according to the Amber alert report. I realize that you probably get many crank calls, but I am telling you that I saw what happened and if we're going to save her, we need to hurry." Joe said heatedly.

"I would like to talk with you in person. Would it be possible for you to come to the Rock Island Police Station, Mr. Adams and talk with me personally?" she requested in that still calm, unexcited tone that Joe thought was inappropriate under the circumstances.

"I was hoping that I could just tell you what I know on the phone and you could go from there."

With a passive authority voice, the Detective said, "From what you have told me, it is obvious that you have knowledge about this case which could be helpful to us. I am also sure that you want to do whatever it takes to protect that little girl. If we together are going to be successful in saving her, we need to move quickly. If you do not agree to come here voluntarily, it will be necessary for me to send an officer to bring you in. It would save a lot of time for you to come here. My name is Detective Judy Martin. I look forward to talking to you, Mr. Adams."

"Okay. I'll be there as soon as I can," Joe said and hung up the phone.

Detective Judy Martin was very stocky, muscular and big boned for a woman. She was not fat at all, but large in stature. And she was tall, probably six feet in height. She had a very warm charming smile, with a twinkle in her green eyes that seemed almost flirtatious. She wore a brown pant suit that fit her perfectly, as though it were tailored. Despite her large size, she was definitely feminine.

"Hello, Mr. Adams. Please follow me. May I call you Joe?"

He followed nervously as she led him to a small, neat, yet somehow uncomfortable room. The only pieces of furniture were a table and four wooden chairs. She pulled out one chair and invited Joe, "Please have a seat." The Detective took a seat across from him and placed a note pad on the table.

While scribbling something on the paper she asked, "Now what is it you know about the abduction of Carol Bridges?"

"I am not sure where to start but I can tell you that I saw it. She was taken in the alley by a man named Pete. He was driving a blue Toyota. He knocked her out and stuffed her in the back seat and she dropped her cell phone. She knew this Pete guy, but didn't want to go with him. I don't know if they were related or not, but I know she knew him because she called him by name."

Detective Martin wrote down his comments on the note pad then stopped abruptly and looked Joe directly in the eye. Joe sensed a look of suspicion on her face and knew her attitude was about to change.

"You were close enough to hear what was said?" Detective Martin asked. "This Pete guy snatched her right in front of you? Can you describe him to me?"

Joe did his best to give a description of the man that he saw take little Carol. She then asked if he had gotten the license number of the car.

"No. It all happened so fast and I was nervous. I wish I had but I didn't think to get it. The car was an older blue Toyota, a four door."

Detective Martin's tone turned sterner "You say that you were so close that you could hear every word and yet you did nothing to stop it. What kind of car do you own, Mr. Adams?"

"There was nothing I could do to stop it." Joe spewed the words out of his mouth frantically. "I saw it happen but I wasn't exactly there."

"Well, what exactly does that mean? We have a witness who said that she was taken by a man in a green Chevrolet. She told us that there was no one else in the alley. So I ask you again, what kind of car do you have, Joe?"

"Wait a minute" Joe said defensively. "I don't own a car. I've got a black Ford truck. The green Chevrolet that the old lady saw was a car parked on 44th Avenue in front of her house. It had a sign on the door that said it was from the Rock Island Township Assessor's office. She got it wrong. She was old and she was very upset."

Detective Martin picked up the ear piece of the black telephone that was sitting on the table.

"The Township Assessor is my sister-in-law. Let's see if they were in the area at the time of the abduction."

Detective Martin leaned back in her chair… dialed a number that she obviously knew well and waited for a response.

"Hi, Donna, How are you? Hey, Donna, was your Assessor's car in the 4500 block of 9th Avenue this afternoon?"

Joe could hear what the person on the other end of the phone was saying.

"I'm fine, thanks. Why would you ask me that?"

"It may be important in solving a crime that happened in that area today. I have someone who said they saw your Assessor's car there."

There was a moment of silence while the person on the other end of the phone paused to think. "Yes, we were measuring a property there today. It only took us about thirty minutes so we weren't there long. I was shocked to hear that a little girl was abducted in that area today but I didn't see or hear anything."

"Thanks honey," Detective Martin said, "I'll explain things to you later but right now I am rather busy. See ya tomorrow night."

Detective Martin hung up the phone leaned back in her chair and stared at Joe without saying anything for a moment.

"I am convinced you were there when Carol was abducted. I can smell alcohol on your breath. Were you drunk when you took Carol? I am sure things just got out of hand and you didn't mean to hurt her. If you cooperate now, I may be able to help you. But I think it's time we stop this silly game and you tell me where she is. Is she still alive?"

Joe was not surprised that Detective Martin suspected him of the abduction. Once he convinced her that he was there, what else was she to think? He also knew that if he tried to explain about going back in time and watching the whole scene play like a bad movie, she wouldn't believe him and a lot of valuable time would be lost arguing. He had only one thing to do. He didn't want to do it but a little girl's life was on the line. He was going to take her back in time with him. She would never believe anything else that he said, until she experienced it herself.

"Please, Detective Martin if you will let me talk without interrupting me, you will soon understand everything."

He took the remote from his coat pocket and placed it on the table in front of him. Detective Martin stood up, folded her arms in front of herself and said, "You've got the floor, Mr. Adams."

"This may look to you like a TV remote but I assure you it is not." Joe began. "It is used to go back in time. I used it to watch the abduction. Now I am going to take you back with me. You need to be aware that you won't be able to do anything except watch what unfolds. You will feel as if you are a spirit and will only be able to view the abduction, as a ghost. No one will be able to see you and you cannot communicate with anyone but me. But I will be there with you. Don't be afraid. We'll be able to get back to the present anytime we want. I hope this room is strong enough to do the job but we need to take that risk. I hope you are ready because here we go."

Before Detective Martin could say anything or react, Joe reached down and pushed the 'enter' button. Joe was standing on the corner of 9th Street and 45th Avenue, looking into the face a very pretty, but a very shocked Detective Martin. He was prepared for the reaction that he got.

"What the hell!" she said in an understandingly shocked tone.

"Easy, easy," Joe replied. "Remember what I told you. You are all right. There is nothing to be afraid of, I promise. Just try to calm down and catch your breath. I know it is hard but you are going to have to trust me."

Detective Martin reached out to grab hold of the street sign to steady herself; her hand went right through it and she fought to stay upright, and keep her balance.

"Are you shitting me? What is this? How did you do that? Hey, where the hell am I?"

Joe knew that he had to get her settled down. He was not sure how to do that but he took her hand and reminded her, as calmly as he could, "Please settle down. You are safe. Nothing can harm you. Please remember the things I told you. Try to accept that you are in a different dimension and go with it. Please Detective Martin, you need to calm down. Carol needs you."

Joe was surprised at how rapidly the Detective seemed to react positively to his words. She looked into his eyes and gently closed her hand around his.

"You can't expect me to accept this but I've got little other choice. If you did something to me, I'll kill you when this is over."

"Please Detective, settle down. You are safe just come with me." Joe said.

Nervously she followed him as they moved down 9th Avenue in the direction of the only parked car on the street.

"See that car? It's the Assessor's car. Read the sign on the side of it. That was the one your witness saw. Joe had not noticed before but there was a woman writing something down or concentrating on something in the driver's seat. We need to go this way."

Detective Martin was shocked to see her sister-in-law sitting in that car, unaware of anything except what she was writing.

He led her along the house; the way he had gone before. They stopped at the side of the garage. Detective Martin looked around. They heard the hum of the lawn mower.

"Look," Detective Martins said. "There's our witness washing windows. Joe had not noticed her the last time he was here.

"Carol will be coming around the corner down there in a minute now. Then a car will come from the other end of the alley. You will see."

Just as before, Carol came walking up the alley talking on her cell phone. As she got to the garage, a car pulled up next to her from the opposite direction.

"Hello, Pete," Carol said to the man in the car.

Everything that happened before was repeated in exactly the same way as Joe and Detective Martin watched. As Pete put Carol into the back seat of the Toyota, Detective Martin said, "Come on, we have got to go with them to find out where he is taking her."

They got in the back seat, next to the unconscious little girl, Carol. As before, the car sped down the alley and around the corner.

At 5th Avenue, Pete made a right turn. He recklessly sped down the avenue to the 92 expressway. He drove to the west side of town, to an area that was made up primarily of old, brick, and closed-down factories. At First Street, he pushed the automatic garage door opener, fastened to his sun visor, and drove through the opened overhead door into one of those abandoned buildings. Joe quickly pushed the 'Reset" button on the remote control.

Joe and Detective Martin were immediately returned to the little room at the Police station.

A very upset Detective Martin shouted at Joe, "Why did you do that? We need to see what happened next!"

"Why?" Joe said. "We know where he took her. He might have raped her. He might have killed her. Whatever he did to her, he has already done it. There is nothing we could have done about it then because we were not there. There is nothing we could do about it now except watch it happen. But he may not have done anything physical to her yet, and if that is true, then time is wasting. You know where she is and you need to do something."

Detective Martin jumped to her feet; pointed her finger in Joe's face and yelled, "I will deal with you later, don't you leave!"

She bolted for the door and was gone in a flash, leaving Joe alone in the room without even taking the time to close the door. He heard her yelling orders and there was a great commotion happening in the outer room as people moved quickly. Then everything was quiet as though there was no one around.

Joe sat in the room alone, not sure what to do. Was he under arrest? After about a half hour of sitting there alone, he realized that nobody was paying any attention to him. He calmly stood up, walked to the front door of the Police Department and left without anyone stopping him. He drove back to the lake hoping that the police got too little Carol before anything bad happened to her. He knew that he had not heard the last from Detective Martin. But she was probably going to be very busy, in the meantime.

It was past midnight when Joe got back to the lake. A note was hand written left on the kitchen table. In what he recognized as an angry tone, it read "Where have you been? Supper is in the oven. Virginia." He fixed himself a drink and sat in the dark at the kitchen table. His nerves had not been this much on edge, since he quit smoking. He really wished he had a cigarette just then. What happened when the police charged the abandoned factory, as he imagined they had done? Did they get there in time? He guessed that he would probably not hear anything until the morning. The TV did not usually cut in with news bulletins in the middle of the night. And then there was Keith. Joe was going to have to call him and let him know that he took a police officer back in time. He really wished that Keith were there advising him. His brother was the smartest person he knew, and the most level-headed. But it would do no good to try to call him so late. He will just have to make it through this night, alone, reviewing his thoughts.

It was seven thirty in the morning when he heard Keith's car pull into the driveway. Without knocking, Keith walked in through the unlocked door. Without saying a word, he grabbed a cup from the cupboard, filled it with coffee, and sat down at the table across from Joe.

"Well buddy, you've done it now; haven't you?" he laughed. "By the way, you look like hell. Did you get any sleep at all last night?"

Surprised by Keith's reaction, Joe said stumbling with his words. "No. I was just too upset. What makes you think that I had anything to do with anything anyway?"

"Your prints were all over that story when I heard it. You should feel better now, knowing that the police found the missing girl, and she is safe. The news didn't say if she was molested or not, but at least she is alive. They got the guy who took her, too."

Joe felt immediately calmed. His brother always had that effect on him. It just never seemed to fail that when something bad happened, Keith was the one with the cool head that held everything together. When life dished out lemons, it was always Keith who made juice out of it, and then added the sugar.

"I am happy Carol is safe and that they got the asshole who took her, I'm glad I did what I did, but now what? The cops are going to be on me like shit on a plumber."

"Settle down! Settle down! What are you worried about? Did you think that you were just going to keep this time travel gizmo all to yourself? One of these days you are going to have to tell Virginia about it and that's where the real fear should come in."

"With what happened the last time we used it," Joe said. "I was thinking about dropping it into the lake."

Keith leaned back in his chair. "You've got to be kidding. I can't believe you're that selfish. I still don't understand how you came up with the plans for this thing, but you did."

"Ya but..." was all that Joe got out before Keith interrupted.

"Ya but my ass! I know that things didn't work out the way you hoped with your dad. I suppose that the truth may have hurt you a little, but the truth is the truth. It didn't pick your pocket or break your bones. So accept it, and grow with it. You came up with probably the greatest invention of the twenty first century. And you wanted to destroy it? Are you crazy?"

"I just didn't think..." Joe started to say before he was again interrupted by his excited brother.

"Come on, Joe, think positively. Look at what you just did. Imagine the things we can do with this thing. You just saved a little girl's life. How many other kids have been lost and never heard from again? How many other things have happened that remain unsolved? When the news of this thing gets out, it could eliminate crime in this world."

"I never thought of it that way, Keith. For some reason I had not considered the positives of time travel, but only the bad. But you are right, there are lots of good things that can come from being able to go back in time and see what really happened in the past. There are so many wrongs that could be righted."

Keith laughed out loud, leaned across the table to look Joe straight in the face and said, "Can you imagine how Detective Martin explained to her superiors how she knew where little Carol was? Wouldn't it be neat to be a little mouse in the corner and listen to her stomp all over herself, trying to tell her boss that she went back in time and saw what happened?"

"You can bet she didn't tell them that, but yes, it would be interesting to hear what she did tell them." Joe said in a more serious tone. "She was pretty upset with me the last time I saw her. I know that I'm going to hear from her again. I'm going to have to figure out how to handle that conversation."

"That's kind of up to you isn't it, Joe? You can do or say anything you want. What's she going to do? Put you in jail?"

"No, she's not going to do that, but she's going to want some answers." Joe said. "I've been thinking about this all night. She's got to be as relieved as I am, about finding little Carol alive and safe. She might have been upset with me, at the time, but I bet she isn't upset about what happened now. I know that I'm going to hear from her again. I don't know what she thinks or what I'm going to do, but I'm not just going to turn this remote over to her. I may be just an old retired plumber, but I know that we've got to do some thinking about how to proceed from here. We… you and I, need to be smart about what to do about her, and what we do next."

Keith slowly rose up from the kitchen chair from which he had been sitting. He crossed his arms in front of himself and with a blank look on his face began pacing around the kitchen. Joe had seen him do this before and knew that he was in deep thought. He was talking to Joe but it seemed like he was really talking to himself. He ranted on for a while and all Joe could do was sit and listen.

"It does cause somewhat of a problem," he began, "that a third person knows about what we've been doing. She knows that time travel is possible because she experienced it herself, and if that isn't enough... she is a cop. I guess the biggest concern is that she is a police officer. But then, she is a cop in Rock Island, Illinois, and as far as she knows, you are 60 miles away in Iowa. She has no authority here. We know that we are going to hear from her, as you say. We can ignore her and refuse to talk to her but that might not be the best thing to do. On the other hand, it might be advantageous to have a police officer help us at some point. I mean, saving that little girl was something that you couldn't have accomplished without police help."

The ringing of the wall phone broke Keith's mood. Both men instinctively knew who was calling him. They stared at each other for a long moment with a look on both men's faces that said, "What do we do, now?"

"Hello, Detective Martin," Joe said calmly. "What can I do for you?"

Keith listened nervously while the person on the other end spoke. Then he heard Joe say "No, I won't go there to talk to you, but you can come here, if you wish."

Keith listened intently to the one sided conversation... Finally, after a long time of Joe listening and not saying anything. He heard Joe say, "You can try to bluff me all you want by telling me that I will come into your police station or you will have me brought in. Let's get this straight. If you want to arrest me for not coming there, then make it happen. Otherwise, if you want to talk about things, then you can come here. I am sure that we can work together, on other crimes, but it will be just that, you and me working together. I look forward to working with you again, but please understand that you are not going to bully me. I don't have to tell you anything and I can deny any claim you might make about time travel. So I hope to see you soon."

"Okay, Joe, I understand." Keith heard Detective Martin say. "Maybe I can bring some steaks up. We can have a cook out and talk things over. I would love to meet your wife."

"That sounds good." Joe said. "Just let me know."

After he hung up the phone, Joe turned to Keith and said. "Our wives have been left out of this whole thing. But if we are going to go further with it, we need to get them up to speed as to what has been happening."

"Virginia is going to kill me" Joe said sheepishly. All of our married lives we have been open and honest about everything. We have had no secrets from each other. She is going to feel hurt, betrayed and angry. She is going to kick my ass when she finds out what we have been doing."

"She already knows." was Keith's comeback. "My wife is the one who heard about little Carol on the news this morning. She jumped into the middle of my butt when I first got up. She, Virginia and Naomi have had their heads together. They put 2 and 2 together and came up with 5jokingly he said. They don't know; well… my wife does know about the time machine; but from what we found out about your father and the way we have been acting, they figured that we were up to something. My wife was so proud of me and I had nothing to do with saving little Carol. According to my wife, Virginia is totally cool with what's going on. But it is time for you to tell her"

Shocked, Joe said. "How could they know anything? We worked so hard at keeping it from them so that they wouldn't worry about us."

"I guess the first clue came from one of your friends who live near you at the lake, calling Virginia about your house disappearing. Apparently the first time we tried the machine, the whole house went back in time."

Joe was so shocked by what he had just heard that he just said nothing and waited for the next shoe to drop.

"I'm not sure if this is the best time to bring this up," Keith said. "We need to decide how and when we are going to make this time travel thing public"

"There are a few things that I need to tell you that you don't know." Keith said. "I didn't build one time machine, I built two. I have one too. I also sent off for a patent to protect us from someone trying to seal this from us. I wasn't trying to deceive you; I just couldn't stand not having one of my own."

Joe settled back in his chair and looked at Keith with a satisfying look on his face. "Why am I not surprised? Knowing you the way I do, I guess that you have gone on a little trip of your own, too, haven't you?"

"Well," said Keith. "Let's just say that I'm a little tired this morning myself. "So, let me get you another cup of coffee while I tell you what I did."

CHAPTER FOURTEEN

"You know Joe that genealogy has been a hobby of mine. I have traced my family on my father's side back to Pocahontas. She was the Indian princess who saved the life of John Smith in Jamestown, in the sixteen hundreds. To refresh your memory of history, the English wanted to colonize the area around Jamestown, for England. The Indians were not too happy about giving up their land to these newcomers, especially when the English couldn't seem to find, or grow enough food to feed themselves. So the Englishmen decided that they would attack Indian villages, kill their woman, children, and steal their food. As you can imagine, the Indian's took this rather personally and decided to fight back. When they did, they defeated the English, and they took their leader, John Smith, as prisoner. As the Indians were about to club John Smith to death, Pocahontas, the chief's daughter, intervened and saved his life.

History books want us to believe that Pocahontas and John Smith were lovers and that was why she saved his life. Some historians suggest that Pocahontas had a little girl's crush on John Smith and that he took advantage of that by having an affair with her. What was pretty obvious from history was that John Smith was a real bad guy. He was supposed to be hung for a number of things he had done, but he always seemed to get out of it somehow. So what was the truth? I am not related to John Smith but I am related to Pocahontas. She was only about twelve years old when the situation with John Smith happened and he was about forty years old. My ancestry goes back to John Rolfe who was married to Pocahontas. They had a child named Thomas who is my ancestor but they had no other children."

Joe looked at Keith in frustration. "What in the hell does this have to do with anything. What's the point? You know that you're an ancestor to Pocahontas, isn't that enough? You're getting long-winded, and I'm getting bored. History books can tell you all of what you've just said. What did you want to find out about?"

"Pocahontas died at twenty-one years of age in England from some kind of fever. She was in fine health one day; she even went to a party the night before she died, according to historical accounts. On the same day that she died, she had a meeting with John Smith. She hadn't seen him in ten years. Her current husband was, John Rolfe. His first wife died at age nineteen from what was supposed to be the same infection of which Pocahontas died, John Rolfe was known to be a very, very jealous man according to his own writings. John Rolfe told Pocahontas that John Smith had died years before they got married. Then she found out that her husband lied to her. Did she confront him about that? Did Pocahontas marry John Rolfe because she thought John Smith was dead? Did they argue over her husband's lies? I wanted to know if Pocahontas died of natural causes, or if she was she murdered by her husband? Most historians believe that her husband did indeed murder her, but that is pure speculation on their part."

Joe smiled at Keith. "Only you would spend your time wondering about something as unimportant as that. Three hundred year old ancestors… are you serious?" It might be neat to find that you are related to Pocahontas, but if her husband killed her, that might not be so neat.

Keith said, "And you didn't wonder about your dad? I always thought it was silly for you to spend so much of your time wondering about that. But it was important to you, so we did all this to get to the truth. My fixations are no less important than yours. We are in the position to answer questions about the past. We can use time manipulation to find the truth about the past. If the truth can be unveiled, then why shouldn't we? If wrongs cannot be righted, then what's the point? These stories of our past are better than most of the Hollywood movies ever made. People who study genealogy don't just want to find the hero's in their family tree. They want to see the whole story, the good, the bad and the ugly, as they say."

"I assume that you got the answers to all of your questions," Joe said. "And I guess that's a good thing for you. But what about the bad sides of this thing we've discovered?"

"Yes I did" Keith answers. "John Rolfe did not kill Pocahontas. I know that for a fact because I saw them with my own eyes. They had gone to a party that King James had held especially for Pocahontas. She was well accepted by everybody at the ball. John Rolfe needed money from the King to help finance his tobacco export business. Pocahontas, who had changed her name to Rebecca, charmed the King into giving her husband the money he needed. She did see John Smith at the ball but was over her crush on him. John Rolfe insisted that he and Rebecca leave the ball earlier than they had wanted because Rebecca started feeling ill. By the next day she had a terrible fever. Their son, Thomas came down with the same fever. Rebecca died from that fever but her son survived after a long illness. That knowledge doesn't make me happy, or sad, but it does satisfy me because I am confident that I know the truth."

"I understand." Joe said. "But some things maybe better left untold."

"What could possibly be wrong with knowing the truth about the past?" Keith asked innocently. "The truth will always prevail. The truth is always good and needs to be known. There is nothing bad that can ever happen from knowing the truth about the past."

"Really…" Joe said. "You're not in church here. I know that you're an optimist but think about it. Are you sure there's nothing in your life that you wouldn't be embarrassed if others knew about it? Would it be okay for your wife, children and friends to know every aspect of your life? You're telling me that you want to know about some ancestor who has been dead for three hundred years. Her death had nothing to do with you, and though it may be interesting what about other things that you don't want to address. How about that? How much do you want known? Does the truth work here for you? How does the truth of that situation from the past help anyone?"

Where does it go? The past only knows, Joe thinks. *Where are we going with this thing and should we really go there? How many tear drops will be created by uncovering unexpected answers to questions that have been put to rest over the course of time? How much pain, suffering and hate will be exchanged for something that changes nothing? Saving the life of Carol seemed to be worth it all. That was a selfless act that proved that our human race can do well. But our humanness often gets in the way. We want to gain knowledge for selfish reasons. But we have come too far now to stop. All good things have a bad side. We need to carefully weigh the outcome of our efforts to gain any real understanding of life... Before we take that giant leap, and go down that path, may we examine the situation fully and may the good outweigh the bad.*

CHAPTER FIFTEEN

Joe opened his eyes and looked at the alarm clock setting on the dresser. He awakened at the same time as he had always done. He had been dreaming something that fascinated him. It seemed so real, yet unfinished. He knew that the memory of this dream would quickly fade. He had dreams that he had wanted to remember before, and as hard as he tried, he couldn't keep them from fading from his memory. He worked desperately to recall it. He faintly remembered that, in the dream, he was in a large room that looked like an attorney's office. There was a large fireplace at one end of the room. A strange looking figure stood in front of the fireplace and was talking without moving his lips. He had a head much too large for his small frame and his eyes were big and very green. Joe tried as hard as he could to remember more of the dream. He was aware that he had a long conversation with the creature and that he was totally comfortable even though he should have been afraid. The memory of the dream was fading fast. The only thing he could now remember was the strange being saying through some kind of thought communication; *well done!*

As he sat at the kitchen table waiting for his wife to get up, he considered what he should do next. He felt as comfortable and confident about the time machine as he had since the day that he and Keith had created with it. It was time for him to tell Virginia everything. He might have to take her on a little trip for her to completely understand but after she went with him, he was confident that she would be as excited about it as he and Keith were. Joe felt that Keith was his partner in this adventure; they had done the entire prerequisite learning together and now they together needed to decide how they were going to proceed. And then, there was Detective Martin. He looked forward to hearing from her again, and solving cold case files together.

It's a pretty day today. Joe thought to himself. *Only good things will come from this time machine. We will see to it. So, let's do it!*

The End